Once upon a Place

Once upon a Place

Compiled by
EOIN COLFER
Laureate na nÓg

Illustrated by
P. J. LYNCH

Little Island

ONCE UPON A PLACE

First published in 2015 by
Little Island Books, 7 Kenilworth Park, Dublin 6W, Ireland

ISBN: 978-1-910411-37-7

A British Library Cataloguing in publication record for this book is available from the British Library.

Designed by Fidelma Slattery

Printed in Poland by L&C Printing

With thanks to The Arts Council / An Chomhairle Ealaíon, The Arts Council of Northern Ireland, Poetry Ireland and the Department of Children and Youth Affairs.

Laureate na nÓg is an initiative of the Arts Council, administered by Children's Books Ireland and with the support of the Arts Council of Northern Ireland, the Department of Children and Youth Affairs and Poetry Ireland.

Laureate
na nÓg

Supported by
The National Lottery®
through the Arts Council of Northern Ireland

10 9 8 7 6 5 4 3 2 1

Dear Reader

It is quite possible that you read the title of this anthology and are now thinking to yourself: *Once upon a Place? Surely that's wrong. Surely that's supposed to be Once upon a time. Everyone knows that. What kind of idiot would get the title of his own anthology project wrong? And this fellow is the Children's Laureate? This moron is representing Irish children's books?*

Yes, I admit it. (Not the moron part, which has never been conclusively proven, as Facebook comments do not constitute proof.) What I am admitting to is that the line usually is *Once upon a time* and not *Once upon a place*, but place is important too, isn't it? Stories have to be set somewhere. *Treasure Island* wouldn't be much of a story without an island that had treasure on it. *Gulliver's Travels* would have been pretty boring without Lilliput to land on. And the Chronicles of Narnia would have been a fairly brief series if there had been nothing at the back of Digory Kirke's wardrobe but fur coats.

So, in my opinion, where a story is set is just as important as when it is set. Especially in Ireland. People often ask me, on my travels: *Why do so many writers come from Ireland?* And I tell them that the clue is in the question. It is because we are from Ireland and this is a magical place.

Now, I know that the phrase 'magical place' is slightly overused and often undeserved. Generally people look back on their younger days and say stuff in pubs like: *Janey, do you remember that beach we went to where there was that chip van? That place was magic.* Often this kind of place is not really magical. Semi-magical at the most. Because we adults tend to get all sentimental about our youths. Rose-coloured spectacles and so forth. If you were to look at an old photograph of that beach, it would probably be a windswept stretch of pebbles with a dirty old unlicensed fast food caravan over by the wall. Now, don't get me wrong. I'm not saying a manky old excuse for a beach can't be magical if you got your first kiss there or better still your first choc-ice, because magic is very good at disguising itself.

But when kids are in a place, and right then at that moment while they are actually there, they often stop whatever shenanigans they are perpetrating and just look around them and think: *This place is not so bad really* – then that place probably is magic.

And there are places like that all over Ireland. I'm sure if you think about it, you could come up with a dozen or so magical spots yourself. Maybe your best friend's garden, or the school handball alley, or the cluster of sockets in the corner of the sitting room where you can play Playstation and charge your phone at the same time. We all have our personal spots. And in this collection some of Ireland's favourite writers are going to tell stories of their magical places. And remember, magic doesn't always have to be all skeleton detectives and fairy police forces and Expecto Patronum; sometimes it can be finding a euro, or meeting a lad who's double jointed or discovering a quiet spot to read your favourite book in. Personally I do like skeletons and explosions but that's just me.

So, if my witty introduction hasn't already persuaded you to read this book, let me further charm you with a taste of the wonders held within. You will read stories of magical pumping stations, adolescent detectives and transforming bears to name but a few. You will be absorbed by wonderful poems which conjure pictures of school holidays, bloodthirsty donkeys and travelling snails. And with every word you read you will be transported to various places around Ireland where magic is as warm and golden as the summer sun.

And by the time you close this book it will probably be very late and you will pull the duvet up around your ears, close your eyes and dream a dream which begins with a deep and wise voice saying the words: *Once upon a place …*

EOIN COLFER
Laureate na nÓg (2014–2016)

Contents

Gren's Ghost

by

MARIE-LOUISE FITZPATRICK

I'm climbing out the window. It's midnight. I step carefully into the flower patch beneath my bedroom window and shine the torch around my feet to avoid damaging my dad's prize-winning gladioli. I lower the window, balancing it on my school ruler so it doesn't close completely. I mustn't get locked out. Ringing the doorbell when I get back is not an option. My mother would never recover from the shock of knowing her one and only son has been wandering the neighbourhood in the middle of the night. My parents think I'm good-as-gold. And usually I am. But tonight I'm climbing out.

When Gren Harrington took me aside in school today and asked me to meet him at the Seven Castles carpark at ten minutes past midnight, I should have said no. But I said yes. Because that's what everyone says to Gren Harrington. I've often watched him from my corner of the classroom and tried to figure out why. I think he may have charisma. I've read the definition – magnetic charm or appeal – and, yup, it fits. I guess that's why when he came up to me in the corridor today and said, 'So, Flynn, the other boys have you down as a bit of a wet blanket but I'm thinking there's more to you than meets the eye. Am I right?' I found myself wanting to nod. But I wasn't at all sure that there was. More to me. Than meets the eye. So I tried a non-committal shrug.

He said, 'I have this thing I want to do but I'll need some help pulling it off. I figure you're my man. What do you say?'

I thought: *What thing? When? Where? What will I have to do? Will it hurt?* I said, 'Sure.'

'Great,' he said. 'You live in Kells, right?

I nodded.

'I live a mile outside,' he said.

As if I wouldn't know that – we travel on the same school bus every day.

'The Seven Castles,' he said. 'You know the visitors' carpark?'

I nodded again.

'I'll see you there,' he said. 'Tonight, ten after midnight. Bring a torch.' He drew his fingers across his lips in a zipping motion and grinned at me before walking away to join his friends. That grin said he knew I'd be there, he knew I wouldn't bottle out.

And even though I've been scared stupid all evening I've never once considered not going. It's only now, as I arrive at the carpark still breathless from stumbling across the fields by torchlight, that it occurs to me this could be some sort of ambush. Maybe there'll be a whole gang of boys waiting for me. Maybe I've been chosen as the victim in some initiation thing where they take turns beating me to a pulp. I stop dead in the lane outside the carpark. *Are you mad or what?* I ask myself.

A hand closes on my arm.

'Get off the road, will you?' Gren Harrington shines his torch in my face and pulls me after him through the gate into the empty parking lot.

'Why are we here?' I ask. I can hardly hear my voice over the roar of blood rushing through my ears. I probably sound as freaked out as I am.

'You'll see,' is all he says. He indicates the ruins in the field below us with his head. 'Come on.'

We cross the tarmac and pass through the stile into the field. I can see cow shapes standing around in the darkness; I suppose they are asleep. *I should be asleep. I should be at home, in my bed, asleep.* The big walls that surround the ruins grow blacker as we near them. The square towers along the walls seem to challenge us: *Come inside if you dare.*

'They're not castles,' I say. 'They're watch towers, meant for defence. We call it the Seven Castles but it's actually a walled priory.'

I'm gabbling, doing my Finbar Swot-face Flynn thing. That's what the boys in school call me – Finbar Swot-face Flynn. *Cut the history lecture, Swot-face,* I tell myself. But I'm afraid if I stop talking my knees will turn to jelly and I'll collapse on the grass. 'You probably know all this stuff already,' I say.

'Not all of it,' Gren says.

There's no sarcasm in his voice and there's no menace in his smile, but I know he's a good actor – I've seen him lie to a teacher without so much as breaking a sweat. One smile doesn't mean our entire class isn't hiding behind those walls, waiting for me.

The ground dips steeply; I try to concentrate on minding my step. Any minute we'll pass under the entrance arch. If someone's lying in wait, this is where they'll be. I want to turn and run; instead I speed up. Whatever it is I've walked myself into, I have to get on with it. I rush right in, swinging my torch around.

Nothing but stones – broken walls, arches, the outlines of what were once churches, buildings and rooms. I stand in the centre of it all, taking deep breaths, giddy with relief.

'Got to hand it to you, man,' Gren says, coming up behind me. 'I find this place creepy. You marched in here like it's the middle of the day.'

He taps my backpack. 'What have you got there?' he asks.

'Just some things I thought might come in handy,' I say.

He jerks the backpack off my shoulders, tests the weight of it, puts it down.

'Let's see then,' he says.

I filled the backpack in my bedroom while I waited for midnight to come. My plan was this: in the event of an emergency, I coolly reach into my bag and take out just what we need; if nothing happens, it all stays in the bag. I packed extra batteries for the torch, a blanket, some rope, chocolate (two large bars), biscuits (Fig Rolls), a map of the site from the Seven Castles' website. I considered a flask of soup but the logistical problems of organising it without arousing the suspicions of my parents were too complex, so instead I brought Cup-a-Soups, an old saucepan, water, sticks and matches. Now I notice Gren has a backpack too. Of course he has. He'll have brought everything he needs for whatever this thing is he wants us to do. I feel my face flush pink as I take all the stuff out of my bag.

'We won't starve then,' Gren says. And winks.

He reaches into his backpack. He pulls out a weird-looking old camera and a load of dark material which I mistake for a blanket until he shakes it out. It's a monk's robe, brown, with a hood.

'Rented,' he says. 'Pascal's Party Shop, Kilkenny. Cost me thirty euros. But it'll be worth it, to see their faces.'

'Whose faces?' I ask. I can't stop myself glancing over my shoulder.

'6A,' he says. 'That mob of muppets you and me are privileged to call our classmates. Tomorrow I plan to go in and tell them a story, one in which I have spent the night alone in the Seven Castles and caught a peek of the famous Priory Ghost.'

'There's a ghost?' I say, glancing around again. 'I've never heard of a ghost.'

'Sure you have,' Gren says. He slings the robes at me. He waves the camera in my face. 'He's appearing tonight and I'll have proof.'

'They'll say you Photoshopped it,' I say.

'It's a Polaroid camera,' he says. 'Which means instant prints.' He points to the slot where the photos come out. 'Can't mess with them. And even if the lads have their doubts, I'll still go down in school history as the boy who spent the night alone in the Seven Castles.'

'You're not alone,' I say.

'Ah, but I am,' he says. 'Tonight you're not Finbar Flynn, you're the Priory Ghost.'

'But then,' I say, 'no-one will ever know …'

'You were here?' Gren says. 'I'll know.' He looks at me questioningly, like he hopes that will be enough.

It is. I nod.

'I looked around the class to pick me the perfect partner for this adventure, and there you were,' he says. 'Let's sort the photos first.'

As I pull on the monk costume Gren suggests I use my rope to tie it around the middle because the cord that came with it looks pathetic. He checks my maps for the most authentic place for a ghost monk to walk. We find the perfect spot. We set up the torches to provide atmospheric shadows. I walk; Gren clicks. Photo after photo slides out of the camera. We line them up and reveal them all at once, peeling off the backing paper, groaning and hooting as we see what we've got. Most of them are useless but two look convincingly spooky.

'Score,' says Gren and punches the air.

'Score,' I say.

The perfect partner for this adventure is me, I think.

We make a small fire with my sticks
and heat the water in the pan,
but we take it off too
early and the soup is
lukewarm-lumpy.
We eat it anyway,
me in the monk
robes and Gren
wrapped   up
in the blanket

I brought. We talk, talk, munch, munch, words and biscuits
and chocolate in the glow of the firelight.

'You know what I think?' Gren says, thumping his
head like he's had a sudden brainwave. 'You
need to drop the bar.'

'Huh?'

'The bar. Secondary school
will be three kinds of hell
with a name like Fin-
bar. Finn Flynn. Now
that's a cool name.'

I consider this.
'But how …'

'Just start using it. Like you mean it. Write it on your schoolbooks and your copybooks. Next time someone asks your name, you'll say ...' He leaves the sentence dangling and stares at me expectantly.

'F-finn,' I say.

'Again,' he says.

'Finn,' I say. 'Finn Flynn.'

'Again,' he says, raising his voice.

'Finn Flynn,' I say, raising mine.

'Again,' he shouts.

'Finn Flynn,' I yell.

Gren jumps to his feet and I scramble to mine.

'Finn Flynn, Finn Flynn, Finn Flynn, Finn Flynn,' Gren chants, and he leads me around the fire, stamping his feet and waving his arms. 'Finbar Flynn is dead and gone, long live Finn Flynn,' he roars.

The words bounce around the fractured walls: 'Finn, Flynn, Finn, Flynn, inn-inn-in.'

We laugh at the echoes, we laugh at our dancing shadows, we laugh at everything-nothing till tears roll down our cheeks and our bellies hurt.

'Gren's a really cool name,' I say when we're done.

'A lot cooler than what it's short for,' he says.

I stop and search about my head, adding endings to his name, trying for a likely match. No. Gren couldn't be short for —

'We need to get gone,' Gren says, handing me my blanket. 'The sun is coming up.'

He's right. The walls of the priory are turning pinky grey. He kicks dirt over the ashes of our little fire and I gather up my stuff.

'Thanks for having the guts to come tonight, Finn,' Gren says. 'You must have wondered what you were getting yourself into. Fair play, man.'

We don't say much as we pass the cow shapes and go through the carpark. In the lane he thumps my arm in salute, and sets off at a run. He's gone.

Does this make us mates? I wonder, as I cross the fields towards home, but I know it doesn't. When he shows the ghost photos to the other boys they'll look around to see who his accomplice was and it'd give the game away if he's suddenly talking to me. He never has before.

The ruler is where I left it. I tilt it slightly, get my fingers underneath the frame and lift the sash. I climb back into my bedroom. Everything seems just as it was. I'll go into school later and no-one will know that Finbar Swot-face Flynn is not a wet blanket. Nobody but Gren.

And me. I'll know. I know.

Finbar Flynn is dead and gone. Long live Finn Flynn.

The Pumping Station

by

RODDY DOYLE

7 September 1968

Kevin ran along Kilbarrack Road. He was alone and normally he wouldn't have been running. It had never really made sense, running, unless it was for football. Running without a ball was usually just stupid.

This time, though, running was necessary.

He ran past the shops.

'You're in a hurry, Kevin,' Mr Butler, the grocer, shouted after him.

'Yeah,' Kevin shouted back, because what Mr Butler had shouted was true.

Kevin was in a hurry. He was going for a swim. The sea was at the top of the road and the tide would be high and perfect, and he had to get back home before his mam found out he was gone.

He was at the part of the road he liked best, especially when he was in his dad's car. It was a gentle hill that hid what was ahead. It was just the houses, until you got very close to the top. Then you saw it – the sea.

But you didn't. That was the thing. The public toilets and the pumping station were in the way. You should have seen Dublin Bay and Bull Island, and you did if you looked to the left or right. But right ahead was the pumping station, a kind of yellow, flat-roofed block.

'What does the pumping station pump?' Kevin had once asked one of the older boys, Harry Delap.

'Shite,' said Harry Delap.

'Really?' said Kevin.

He blushed a bit, and laughed. He could feel the heat in his cheeks. He hated that – when he blushed.

'Serious?'

'All the pooh from all over the northside of Dublin,' said Harry Delap. 'Every number two and an ocean of number ones.'

Kevin's mam said Harry Delap was too smart for his own good and his dad always said he was a proper little bowsie. But Kevin thought Harry Delap was brilliant, although he was a bit frightened of him too. Harry Delap was mad. He'd once set fire to his own schoolbag so he wouldn't have to do his homework.

Kevin ran past the big house with the orchard. He was at the top of the road now, where it joined the main road to Howth. There were no cars near, so he ran across to the pumping station. His mam had told him never to go swimming alone and never, ever – ever – to jump off the roof of the pumping station into the sea – ever. And that was what he was going to do now. He was going to get up on the roof and jump.

There were concrete steps down to a platform behind the station. In the winter and when it was windy, the tide came up over the platform and even up the steps. But there was no wind today and the waves weren't big or angry. He took off his clothes and put on his togs. He covered himself with his towel just in case someone came down the stairs – especially a girl. He put his runners back on. He needed them, to climb up onto the roof of the pumping station.

All his friends had done it. They'd climbed and jumped. But Kevin hadn't. All that summer, they'd climbed and jumped. Except Kevin. Because his mam had told him not to. Now, a week after the end of the summer holidays, he was going to do it. He didn't care that none of his friends would see him. He just wanted to do it, to get it into his head: *I jumped off the roof, into the sea.*

He ran at the wall beside the steps. He jumped and grabbed the top and pulled and climbed up, and stood on the ledge. On one side of him were the steps; on the other, lower down, were rocks and sea and rats. He couldn't see any rats but he knew they were there because he'd seen them before.

He walked along the wall, up along the ledge, till he came to the top. Now he was at the hard bit. He had to jump from the wall to the roof. He'd tried it before and he'd fallen. His elbow had whacked the wall and he'd landed on his bum. He'd had to pretend that it wasn't the most painful and embarrassing thing that had ever happened to him.

He could feel the sea and rats behind him, he could see the drop in front of him.

He jumped.

His fingers – a hand, then his other hand – gripped the roof. He pulled, and got an elbow, both elbows, onto the ledge. He pulled and groaned, and rose, and rolled up onto the roof.

He'd made it.

Now he had to jump.

He looked down. The platform, and his clothes, were right below him. The platform was wide. There was a metal railing running along it. If he didn't jump out far enough, he'd bang his head off the railing and he'd be dead before he hit the water, and he wouldn't go straight to heaven because he was disobeying his parents and he'd laughed when Harry Delap had said 'shite'.

He stopped looking down and walked back to the other side of the roof. Anybody walking or driving past could see him. He didn't care.

He took deep breaths.

He ran – one, two, three, four.

He jumped.

He was in the air – way over the platform and the railing.

Down.

He was in the sea, under the water. He kept his legs up, so his feet wouldn't smash into the stones and rocks. He rose back up, his head burst into the air, he shook the water from his face and shouted, 'Yes!'

He'd done it. He'd *done* it. He was looking out at the sea and Bull Island.

He turned.

The pumping station was gone.

He rubbed his eyes and looked again. The pumping station, the platform, the steps, his clothes – they weren't there. Everything else seemed the same but that just made it stranger, and scarier.

'Where's it gone?'

He swam to where the pumping station should have been. He still expected it to appear. The sun and the sea had been in his eyes – *there* it was.

But it wasn't there. It had vanished. There wasn't a sign that it had ever been there.

He climbed up over the rocks. He was shivering – he was cold and scared. He got onto the path.

The cars! There were millions of them, way more than he'd ever seen. There were two long lines of them, going to Howth or into town. He'd never get across the main road.

Traffic lights! There were new traffic lights. He didn't know when they'd been put there. The cars had loads more colours than usual too, and some of them were huge. It was like being in a film.

The cars stopped and Kevin ran across, to Kilbarrack Road. The old house and the orchard were gone. There was a big block of flats there now.

He ran. His runners were full of water and he was only wearing his bathing togs but he didn't care. He had to get home. He wanted his parents to explain what was happening.

Kilbarrack Road seemed the same.

But it wasn't. Some of the houses were gone and a lot of them were different. There were new colours, new windows. There were new houses behind the old cottages. There were cars parked everywhere.

He came to the shops.

Mr Butler wasn't there and his shop wasn't there. It was a chipper. He liked Mr Butler – where was he? Where was Mrs Butler? The sweet shop was gone. It was something called a Centra. The door slid open when he was running past it. It *slid*.

The chemist was different. The butcher's was a place for buying wine and beer!

The last houses before his house were different too. The garages had been changed into rooms with big windows.

And Flood's farm across the road was gone. There were houses there, hundreds of them. Where were all the Floods?

He was nearly at his own house now. Right ahead of him, where the road narrowed and became a lane with the hedges and fields on both sides – that was different now too. The road was wide, the hedges were gone. There were more houses – and a factory.

He came to his house. The gate was bigger and there was another gate at the side of the house. It was locked. He couldn't go around the back to the kitchen, the way he always came and went.

What was going on?

He went to the front door. It was different too. There were *two* front doors!

He looked in the front window. The venetian blinds that should have been there were gone. There were people in there, in the sitting room, people Kevin had never seen before.

He yelled. It was the sound of his fright escaping. He leaned down and got sick. He couldn't help it. He breathed – in, out. He rubbed his face with his hands. He stood up straight – and looked again.

There was a very old man sitting in a big chair. He was laughing. There was an old woman. She was really small and she was laughing too. There was another man. He was about the same age as Kevin's dad, maybe older. He had glasses a bit like his dad's, and his hair was grey and short. There were two teenage girls and a boy. There was another woman. Kevin didn't know any of them. He'd never seen them before.

But –

They all looked familiar.

Kevin looked at each face.

The boy looked a bit like Kevin. The man looked like his dad. The old man –

The old man *was* Kevin's dad! He was definitely Kevin's dad. It was mad but Kevin knew it was true. The old man was Kevin's dad and the boy was Kevin's son – and the grey-haired man in the middle was Kevin!

Kevin wanted to run.

The old lady was his mam and the teenage girls were his daughters and the other woman must have been his wife!

Yeuk!

He looked again. She looked nice.

What was happening now?

They were fading. They were all fading. No – not all of them. Kevin the adult and his children, his wife – they were starting to disappear. His parents, the old people, weren't fading – and they weren't smiling.

The old man, his dad, was looking straight at him. His mouth opened – one word. Kevin shouldn't have heard it, but he did. Clearly.

'Quick!'

He knew what he had to do.

He ran.

Back.

Back past the houses, past the strange shops, past all the mad-looking cars. He passed loads of people. He didn't know them and no-one seemed to see him. He had to get back into the sea – he just knew he had to.

He ran across the main road. He ran over the path.

The sea was in front of him. He dashed down, over the rocks, into the sea. He kept going, kept swimming, till it felt deep enough. Then he dropped his head under the water and pushed and kicked and made sure all of his body was under. He stayed under as long as he could. He held his breath till he thought he'd explode – his lungs, his head, all of him would explode and vanish. Then he let himself rise.

He opened his eyes, shook his head. The sea was there, and Bull Island.

He turned. He didn't want to, but he had to.

He turned and looked.

It was there, it was back.

'Yes!'

The pumping station was back. He could see his clothes in a pile on the platform.

He got dressed without bothering to dry himself first. It was harder to get dressed when you were wet, but Kevin didn't care.

He ran up the steps. He loved those steps.

The new traffic lights were gone. The old house was back, and the orchard.

He ran.

Back down Kilbarrack Road, past the shops.

'You're still in a hurry, Kevin,' Mr Butler shouted.

'Hiya, Mr Butler!'

Kevin kept running. He didn't think he'd ever stop.

But he would.

He'd stop when he got home.

The Cabin in the Woods

(Co Wexford)

by

ENDA WYLEY

There's the Doberman –
as startled by us
as we are by her,
standing hip-high
in the damp black grass.

There's the cabin
with its rain tank,
its wood pellet stove,
its solar lights
and bamboo walls.

There's yesterday's
ghosts chattering
like magpies
and there's the forest
rich with mud paths.

In the plots close by
the young trees sigh
their late summer sighs
and lights are draped
like washing over the terrace.

And there's us –
wild haired,
with dirty finger nails.
We're city guests
awed by the quiet.

Then sleep comes
like a warm blanket,
until night's fox
is chased away
and morning is the dog
that scratches at our door.

Time to gather
the breakfast eggs.
Time to swing
on the hammock.
Time to pluck grass
for the indolent horses.

Time to live
for ever like this –
children in bare feet,
amber necklaces
in the sun
our lucky charms.

The Bear

by

JOHN CONNOLLY

The bear appeared shortly after they arrived in Kerry. Steven was surprised to see it, mainly because there weren't supposed to be any bears in Kerry, or not any that he knew of. Of course, it was possible that the bear was the last of its kind and had been keeping a low profile for fear of being sent to a zoo or – worse – shot. If so, it must have been a pretty remarkable bear, because it wasn't as if there were many places for a bear to hide in Ballylongford. As far as Steven could tell, the whole area was short on caves and woods, which was where he understood most bears liked to live.

Steven hadn't been anticipating the appearance of a bear at their new home. In fact, he hadn't been anticipating very much at all. His newly reduced family – his mum, his brother David and him – had come down to Kerry to live in their grandmother's old house after their dad left. It was the start of the summer holidays, so school wasn't a problem. His mum said that she just wanted a little time to think. Steven thought that she missed his dad. He didn't know why his dad had gone away. He felt that his dad didn't want to leave, and his mum didn't really want him to go either, but everything between his parents had become angry and confused, and now they were down to three.

Their grandmother had been dead for a couple of years. Steven couldn't remember much about her, because he'd been only little when she died. The house had mostly been standing empty ever since, except when his mum or one of her sisters decided to use it for a holiday. It was dusty and smelt of old clothes, but the fields behind it stretched for miles and the sun shone more brightly than it did in the city.

A few days before the bear came, Steven found a book on the shelves entitled *500 Fascinating Facts about Kerry!* It was written by someone named A. Mohan. The book was very odd. To begin with, A. Mohan seemed to struggle to find 500 fascinating facts about Kerry and so had settled for 499. A. Mohan also seemed to have a strange idea of what a fact might be.

FASCINATING FACT NO. 17:
KERRY IS THE ONLY COUNTY IN IRELAND TO HAVE THE SAME LETTER OCCURRING TWICE IN SUCCESSION IN ITS NAME.

Hang on, thought Steven, *that's not right. What about Roscommon, and Offaly? What about Derry, and Kilkenny?*

FASCINATING FACT NO. 97:
KERRY IS CORK SPELT BACKWARDS.

Seriously?

FASCINATING FACT NO. 123:
KERRY WAS ONCE PART OF GIBRALTAR.

Now wait a minute ...

FASCINATING FACT NO. 156:
KERRY ONCE BOASTED THE HIGHEST
MOUNTAIN IN IRELAND, CARRAUNTOOHIL,
UNTIL THE DISCOVERY OF MOUNT TULLY IN
COUNTY KILDARE.

Steven knew for certain that Kildare was the flattest county in Ireland. If a man stood on a chair in Kildare, you could see him on the horizon, never mind unexpected mountains suddenly appearing out of nowhere. Steven had thus begun to view *500 Fascinating Facts about Kerry!* with a degree of caution, even mild concern. He suspected that A. Mohan might be mad.

David, Steven's brother, was older than him by three years. Ever since they'd arrived in Ballylongford, David had started bringing odd creatures into the house: earwigs that he kept in a glass case in his bedroom and to which he gave the names of Roman emperors; a three-legged mouse that quickly vanished through a hole in the floorboards no wider than a pencil, and could occasionally be heard running behind the bookshelves, as though desperately trying to find the way out again; and a fat pigeon that David claimed was unable to fly, but which turned out simply to be lazy. After a short nap and a peck on some breadcrumbs, the pigeon suddenly appeared to realise that wherever it was, it wasn't where it was supposed to be, and flew headfirst into the window, knocking itself out for a time. David had even briefly managed to bring a squirrel home, which was no mean feat. Squirrels are nervous animals and it's hard to get them to go anywhere they don't want to, but somehow David convinced the squirrel to come into the house, whereupon, like the pigeon, it quickly began to panic and ran around knocking things over and generally making a nuisance of itself.

They were all quite relieved when the squirrel left.

FASCINATING FACT NO. 199:
KERRY WAS ONCE RULED BY THE BADGER
KING, UNTIL HE WAS OVERTHROWN BY THE
OTTER PRINCE.

But bringing home a bear was another thing entirely, especially when their mum was out. Their mum had left them with a lot of instructions about how to behave when they were alone in the house. These included, but were not limited to: not turning on the oven; not turning off the oven if it was already on; not opening the door to strangers; not talking to strangers even through a closed door; and not climbing on any object more than six inches high. Admittedly, she had not supplied any rules about not bringing bears into the house, but Steven was quite sure that this fell under the general heading of not having things to do with strangers.

Steven was lying on the living-room floor, colouring a picture, when David arrived with the bear. He was holding the bear by the paw, or the bear was holding him by the hand. Either way, he and the bear were hand-in-paw.

Steven put down his crayon.

'It's a bear,' he said, although this was pretty obvious and really didn't need remarking upon.

'I know,' said David.

'Where did you find it?'

'In the field behind the house.'

'What was it doing?'

'Just standing there.'

'Maybe it was waiting for someone.'

'Who would a bear be waiting for?'

Steven considered the question. 'Another bear?'

'I don't think he was waiting for another bear. I think he was waiting for one of us.'

'How do you know it's a he?'

'I just do.'

Steven didn't know how you went about telling a male bear from a female bear. He wasn't sure that he wanted to know either. However you did it, he didn't think the bear would be too happy about the whole business.

Steven regarded the bear. It wasn't really like any bear that he'd ever come across in photographs or on TV or even in the zoo. It was more like a teddy bear than an actual bear. Its fur was golden brown, but thin and worn in places. Its eyes were glassy, like buttons, and one ear was torn. It was also wearing a red and white spotted tie, which was in itself unusual. Steven had never seen a bear wear a tie before.

'Hello,' said Steven, in the absence of anything else to say to a bear.

The bear waved a paw in greeting.

'He seems friendly,' said Steven. He was quite relieved. There was no telling what an unfriendly bear might do. 'Do you think he's hungry?' he said.

'I haven't asked,' said David. He looked up at the bear. 'Are you hungry?'

The bear shook his head.

'Apparently not,' said David.

'What do bears eat anyway?' said Steven.

'Berries, I suppose,' said David. 'Nuts. Fish, too. And honey.'

'Like Winnie-the-Pooh.' Steven was very fond of Winnie-the-Pooh.

'Yes, just like him.'

The bear released his hold on David's hand, sat down in an armchair and gazed at the ghost of himself in the television screen.

'He doesn't say a lot,' said Steven.

'I don't think bears are big on conversation.' David sat beside Steven on the floor.

Together they watched the bear. He wasn't doing much, but he seemed fascinated by his own reflection. Maybe he had never seen himself before, thought Steven, or perhaps he believed that he was looking at another bear entirely. Steven hoped that the bear wouldn't attack the television. They didn't have a lot of money, and he wasn't sure that they could afford to replace it.

'Should we call someone?' he asked.

'Who?'

'I don't know, but his owner may be worried about him. He might have wandered off from a zoo or a circus. Or maybe he was being held prisoner, and managed to escape.'

Steven had a vision of the bear digging a tunnel, or scaling a wall, while searchlights scanned the darkness for him and a siren wailed.

'If he's escaped, then he'll want to keep a low profile,' said David.

Steven didn't think the bear could keep a low profile. He was, after all, a bear. He could possibly get rid of the necktie, which would make him harder to distinguish from other bears, but he would still be a bear.

'We should call the police,' said Steven.

'If we call them, they'll come and take him away.'

The bear shook his head, as if to say that he really didn't want them to call the police, which seemed to decide the matter. They all remained silent for a while.

'Mum will be angry that you brought a bear home,' said Steven. 'The squirrel was bad enough.'

'But she hasn't met him yet. She might like him.'

Steven was almost certain that their mother wouldn't approve of the bear. She didn't even want them to get a puppy. He hoped that he wouldn't get into trouble for being party to letting the bear into the house. If it came down to it, he'd have to tell her that it was David who'd brought the bear home.

'He might like to watch television with us,' Steven suggested.

He was, to be honest, getting a little bored with just looking at the bear. The bear wasn't doing a lot. For a bear, he was pretty uninteresting, once you got over his basic bearness.

'OK,' said David.

He turned on the television, and together they and the bear watched some cartoons, and a documentary about salmon – which the bear appeared to enjoy a lot – and then a war film. The war film was a bit violent, so after half an hour the bear changed the channel back to more cartoons.

FASCINATING FACT NO. 397:
IF YOU SHOUT YOUR NAME INTO THE MOUTH
OF KERRY'S FAMOUS CRAG CAVE, THE ECHO
ALWAYS COMES BACK AS 'PARDON?'

It was growing dark and starting to rain when their mother's car pulled up outside. They heard her footsteps on the path and her key turning in the door. Steven's tummy gave a little lurch of concern.

Their mother walked into the living room. She looked at the bear. The bear looked back at her. She was carrying a bag of shopping in her hand, which she set down on the table. She was a little surprised to see the bear, but she didn't scream or shout, as Steven was afraid she might, and she didn't appear angry.

'Who's this?' she asked.

'He's a bear,' said David. 'He doesn't have a name, though. Not yet.'

'David brought him home,' said Steven, just to put himself in the clear in case their mother did decide to turn nasty. 'But he's not dangerous,' he added. 'He just sits quietly. He's no trouble.'

He was already getting used to having the bear around. It was like he was meant to be there.

'And where did he come from?' asked their mum. She was staring quite intently at the bear.

'I just found him outside, standing in a field,' said David. 'He looked lonely.'

'Yes,' said their mother. 'I expect he was.'

'Can he stay?' asked David.

'No, I'm afraid the bear has to go.'

Steven wasn't too surprised to hear this, although he would be sad to see the bear leave. But David began to cry.

'I want him to live with us,' he said.

'He can't, not here.'

'But where will he go?'

'That's for the bear to decide.'

She spoke in that tone of voice, the one that wouldn't put up with any nonsense. The bear understood. He wasn't stupid. He rose to leave, and David stood too. He put his arms around the bear.

'I'm sorry,' said David.

The bear patted him on the head. Steven reached out and shook the bear's paw.

44

'Goodbye,' he said. 'It was nice to meet you.'

The bear nodded in agreement, and walked to the front door. He stood for a moment beside their mother, and it seemed that he might have tried to say something to her, were it not for the fact that he was a bear, but the only sound to be heard was David's sobbing.

The bear left, and their mother watched him go.

'Right,' she said, once the front door had closed behind the bear. 'Help me to put away this shopping, and I'll get started on dinner.'

FASCINATING FACT NO. 428: KERRY PRONOUNCED BACKWARDS IS 'REE-KE', WHICH IS ALSO ITS JAPANESE NAME, AND TRANSLATES AS 'SMALL LONELY BIRD'.

They ate in the kitchen. Steven tried to make conversation, but David wouldn't speak, and barely touched his food. They cleared the table, and their mother went to her room. The two boys sat at the living-room window and stared out into the night. The bear was sitting on the garden wall, illuminated by the lights of the house and the beams of passing cars. He sat with his back to them. It was still raining, and his fur was soaking wet.

Their mother appeared from the back of the house and walked across the garden to where the bear sat. She had put on a coat, but her head was uncovered, and the raindrops ran like tears down her cheeks. She spoke to the bear, although the boys could not hear what she said. The bear turned to listen to her. She put her hand to his face and stroked his torn ear. The bear reached up and removed his head, and now the rain fell on their father and mother both.

Their mother returned to them. Their father was gone. They had watched him walk off into the night, his head restored to his shoulders, so that he was a bear once more. The rain had stopped and the moon shone through the clouds.

Their mother sat with her boys, an arm around each of them.

'Will the bear come back?' David asked her.

'Maybe,' she said. 'The bear and I will talk again, and we'll see.'

FASCINATING FACT NO. 500:

THERE ARE BEARS IN KERRY.

Bus
(James Fintan Lalor Avenue, Portlaoise)

Stop

by

PAT BORAN

The world is full of beautiful places;
this is not one of them. Decades back
a line of trees stood here, a gate,
and open fields I half-remember
from a morning walk, the world spread out
and, in that early light, all glistening.

But time moves on, the land
bends to our will. Where cattle dreamt,
now townsfolk come to meet, to shop,
and, like me here, to stop and wait
inside half a wind-swept, glass-walled hut
for the wheels of change
to carry them away. We would be
anywhere some days
but where we are.

And yet last week,
as I sat on this backside-numbing bench
doing little more than breathe, a man
right there beside me took a call.
'Sheila?' His voice was quivering.
'What's that? You're in the clear?
Oh Sacred Heart of Christ,' he said. 'Thank God!'
And before I might do anything, he'd reached
across and hugged me, held me, his ageing fingers
trembling now like grass, his face against mine
damp – and I can feel it still – as early mist.

Abseiling

or The Dancing Engineers

by

SIOBHÁN PARKINSON

(In memory of my father)

This was how Dad began the story: 'Once upon a place, there was a spider.'

'I *hate* spiders,' Sophie squealed. 'They bite you *dead*.'

'Not in Ireland,' said Dad.

They were in Ireland, of course. In Bray, County Wicklow, as a matter of fact. On the beach, under Bray Head. It was one of their favourite places. Sophie liked the promenade best with its blue and orange railings and the tent-shaped ice-cream kiosk second best and the tent-topped bandstand third. Lottie liked the stones best and the sand second and the blue smell and crack of sulphur at the Bumpers third. Dad liked the water and swimming best and teaching his girls to swim. But it was too cold for swimming today, though the sun shone bright in the wide blue sky.

'*Anywhere!*' shrieked Sophie. 'It doesn't matter where you are. You die stone dead if a spider bites you. Tell us a different story, Daddy. Put flying in it.'

'What kind of a place?' said Lottie. 'I mean, what kind of a place was the spider once upon?'

'It doesn't matter where,' Sophie said to her sister. 'Spiders are horrible everywhere.'

'Was it under a stone?' Lottie asked Dad. She liked stones.

'No,' said Dad, 'it was in Bray. Right here. On the beach. But not under a stone.'

'Oh, no!' shouted Sophie. 'Not the *beach*! I can't EVER come here again if the beach has spiders in it. Ever, *ever*, EVER, till I am an Old Woman. *Eeeeek!*' She was, as you will have noticed, a noisy girl. 'They have too many furry arms.'

'I don't think you could have a spider on the beach,' said Lottie, who was good at ignoring Sophie. It was a survival skill. 'They are not seaside creatures, Daddy.'

'Well, I once saw a
ladybird in a cathedral,' Dad said.
'So I don't think a spider on a beach is
all that amazing.'

'And it's not arms, Sophie,' Lottie went
on. 'That's octopuses. Spiders have *legs*.'

'And *teeth*,' hissed Sophie. (Which, by
the way, is not true.)

'What was the spider doing on the
beach, Dad?' asked Lottie, who was good at
the story game, which means asking the right
questions of the storyteller.

'It was lost,' Dad said. 'It had found itself a fine
place to spin a wonder-web, between two feathery
bony structures, but what the spider didn't know was
that the feathery things were wings. It worked that out
pretty quickly, though, when the eagle woke up,
stretched its wings and broke the spider's carefully con-
structed fly-trap.'

'Did it try to repair the damage?' Lottie asked. 'To the web, I mean.'

'No,' said Dad, 'no point in that. With every wing-beat, the web would only break again. So instead the spider crawled around under the eagle's chest and abseiled down the wind on a thread of gossamer and landed on Bray beach – because the eagle had of course been flying to the Eagle's Nest on Bray Head.'

'What kind of an eagle?' asked Lottie.

'What's "abseiled"?' asked Sophie.

'Golden,' said Dad to Lottie. 'Swung down on a rope,' he added to Sophie. 'Only in this case not exactly a rope but a fine thread of spider gossamer.'

'I don't believe this story,' said Sophie.

'Stories are not for believing,' said Dad.

'Are there Golden Eagles in Ireland?' asked Lottie.

'There is a Golden Eagle in this story,' said Dad. 'And this story is in Ireland. So yes.'

'I'd love a Golden Eagle,' said Lottie. 'Not for a pet, just to watch.'

She spread her arms out and did a swoop and a loop and a zoom and a dive and landed on the sand. She folded her wings and looked up at Dad for the next bit of the story.

'I wouldn't,' said Sophie. 'Not if it had spiders spinning in its wings. I'd say a Golden Eagle could *kill* you.'

'Very unlikely that it would want to,' said Dad.

'Swans can kill you,' said Sophie. 'And sharks and whales and bulls and jellyfish and piranhas and tigers.'

'Cars kill people,' said Lottie sourly. 'But you don't mind those. And guns.'

'Anyway, this spider was called James,' said Dad, 'and he was on Bray beach and he was mighty hungry because Bray beach is not a great place for flies. And the ones that are there are the salty kind, which were not to his taste *at all*.'

'Like peanuts,' said Lottie, who only liked the ones in the shells, not the ones in the packets.

'Exactly,' said Dad.

'So how did he get food, this James?' Lottie asked.

'Well, that was the puzzle,' said Dad. 'He was hunched there with his eight knees bent against his two ears, trying to work out where his next meal was coming from, when –'

'When *what*?' asked Sophie.

'I don't know,' said Dad. 'I haven't made up that part of the story yet.'

'That's no good,' said Sophie. 'You can't just stop in the middle of the story.'

'I'm not stopping,' said Dad. 'I'm just taking a thinking break.'

The girls waited for the thinking break to be over, but it went on and on and on and in the end, Lottie said, 'You could make an island out of stones.'

'What for?' asked Sophie.

'To dance on,' said Lottie, starting to pile up some of the large grey cobbles that strewed the sand.

Sophie added some more stones and said, 'The top has to be smooth for the dancing, so we have to choose the flattest stones for that.'

They danced on their stone island for a while and then they dug to Australia for a while, but they'd done that before and they knew already that you only get to damp sand, not to anywhere with kangaroos, so they gave up before too long. Then they buried Dad. That was the best part of the day so far.

'*When,*' Dad suddenly went on, unburying himself, 'the eagle came flying away from Bray Head and landed on a stone island on the beach that some wonderfully inventive engineers had built.'

'That's us!' said Lottie. She loved it when Dad put them in the stories. 'We're engineers, Sophie. Dancing ones.'

'So the eagle said to the engineers –'

'It *talks*?' asked the two girls together.

'Only Eaglish,' said Dad. 'It's an uneducated sort of an eagle. But luckily engineers learn Eaglish at school.

'So anyway the eagle said, "We could fly to Bray Head and look out to sea all the way to the Head of Howth, where the lighthouse winks at me all night long. I fancy he's a little in love with me, to be honest.'"

'We couldn't,' said Lottie. 'We'd be too heavy for the eagle.'

'You would fly by chairlift,' said the eagle. 'And I would fly by wind and air.'

'Chairlift?' asked the girls. They knew about the old chairlift at Bray Head but as far as they knew it hadn't worked for years.

The eagle winked at them like a lighthouse and said, 'Follow me,' and before you could say Jack Robinson, Sophie and Lottie were strapped, side by side, into a thing like a fairground ride. A great iron strut, all yellow and rusty, loomed over them like an ossified giraffe, and suddenly the chairlift drifted silently, gently, up and away over the railway line and the sweep of the bay and they could see the tent-shaped kiosk way down below and the flared conical hat of the bandstand

and, down on the beach, Dad sat hunched by a stone island and waved up at them and their hair was in their mouths with the wind and then they were gliding and gliding on the air.

'We're *flying*,' said Sophie, the chief engineer.

'Look, *puffins!*' cried Lottie, the second engineer, in charge of beach choreography, though they were probably only gulls.

At the top they got out of the chairlift and met the eagle, who was grooming her glorious wing feathers and muttering to herself. 'Spiders. Millions of them. Baby ones. Eugghhh! Under every blinking feather. It's an *infestation*.'

'I forgot all about James,' said Lottie.

'I wish you hadn't reminded me,' said Sophie, wrinkling her nose.

'I wonder if he's found anything to eat yet,' said Lottie.

'I hope not,' said Sophie. 'Look at the hotel down there, the Esplanade. It's like a far pavilion, isn't it?'

'Is it?' said Lottie. 'My! Isn't it wonderful up here! Everything looks different. You can see the roofs of things.'

'And the shapes,' said Sophie. 'The hotel's got little conical tent-roofs on top of it, I never knew that, just like the kiosk and the bandstand. It's like they're all relations.'

There was a ghostly green building, all grimy glass and inside it were some broken chairs and scrawbs of torn floral wallpaper. 'The Eagle's Nest' it said over the door.

Lottie put her head in and the verandah smelt of mould.

'Do you live here?' Sophie said to the eagle, pointing at the building.

'Certainly not,' said the eagle. 'I'm just a tourist here, same as yourselves.'

'We're not tourists,' said Sophie indignantly. 'We live on the Putland Road.'

The eagle looked unimpressed. It was *eating* a spider.

'It's long past tea time,' said Sophie, squinting at her watch, which was new and shiny but hard to read in bright sunshine. 'We'd better be going.'

'Suit yourselves,' said the eagle and crunched on another spider that it had found in its oxter. Its legs weren't furry at all.

So the girls sat back into the chairlift and waved to the eagle and they abseiled, *wheeeee*, all the way back down to sealevel.

They found their dad on the beach where they had left him, lounging in a deckchair and with a newspaper spread across his face.

Lottie lifted the paper and waved her hand in front of her dad's nose to wake him up. 'We were at The Eagle's Nest,' she said. 'The eagle took us. No, I mean, sent us. In the chairlift.'

'Some story,' said their dad with a yawn. 'I don't believe a word of it.'

'Stories are not for believing, Dad,' said Lottie primly.

'Prove it,' said Dad. 'Prove you were up Bray Head.'

Sophie and Lottie thought for a moment and then Lottie remembered something.

'There are cone-shaped hats on the Esplanade roof, we could see them from the top. It is like a far pavilion.'

'By gum,' said Dad. 'By gor and by gum, you are a right pair.'

'Did James find any flies, Dad?' asked Lottie.

'Who is James?' said Dad.

Sophie looked at Lottie and Lottie looked at Sophie and they shrugged.

'We abseiled down, Dad,' said Sophie. 'On a gossamer thread. Like spiders.'

She didn't even shriek when she said the word 'spiders', Lottie noticed.

'Well, isn't that a wonder!' said Dad, and he stood up out of his striped deck chair and rolled up his newspaper. 'We're late for tea and there is sand in my pockets. That's a nice how-d'ye-do, isn't it?'

And overhead a Golden Eagle spread her wondrous wings across the sky and flew off over the bay towards Howth to visit her winking admirer, the Baily Lighthouse.

Beautiful Dawn

by

PAULA LEYDEN

The story you are about to hear might strike you as a little strange. Perhaps, if you are the sceptical type, you'll think it is a tale made up. You are of course entitled to your opinion, but I am obliged to tell you that you are wrong. These events, which unfolded along the River Nore in the summer of 2014, all happened. You'll probably wish they hadn't. I do too, but wishing never did anyone any good, no matter what you've been told. So, wish away if it brings you a little peace, I won't deny you that, but know this: during these warm and gentle months something strange was afoot along this Kilkenny waterway. Something that caused the horses to twitch and dance in the moonlight and made the dandelions shake their delicate heads as the cattle huddled, perplexed, in the ditches far from the banks of the river. We will leave them there as I introduce you to young Kitty O'Brien.

The very first day of the summer holidays was a day made in heaven. The sky was painted a proper blue and the breeze that ruffled Kitty's open curtains was soft. As she lay in bed, half asleep, she heard a strange sound at the window.

Scrape, scratch.

Scrape, scratch.

Kitty lives in a small farmhouse along the banks of the River Nore, right on the edge of Kilkenny. For those of you unfamiliar with Kilkenny, it is an ancient city in Ireland and this particular river runs through it. The city is famed for its magnificent hurlers, its very own ghost – Dame Alice Kytler, a witch, a murderer and a faithless employer – and its castle. Young Kitty has lived on the farm for all of her thirteen years on this earth. She is tall and talkative and has two best friends. One of them is called Chessie and she is a shaggy brown horse. The other is Sam. He's a human.

So, back to the scratching and scraping.

Kitty lay there for a while when she heard the noise. It didn't worry her at first, as there was a tall ash tree just outside her window and in high winds one of the branches would knock against her window pane. But it did start to worry her when she listened for the wind and found there was none.

The noise got louder and she sat up and reached for her glasses. As she peered out of the window she saw, at the top of the tree, a boy in a blue T-shirt. He was standing there rocking the branches backwards and forwards.

Kitty froze. As you would.

The boy became still and tilted
his head as he stared at Kitty. He
made no sound.

Now, Kitty is not a person easily frightened.
If you saw her on the back of her beloved horse,
leaping over ditches and galloping under low-lying branches,
you would realise that. But her heart did start beating a little
faster as she stared at the boy.

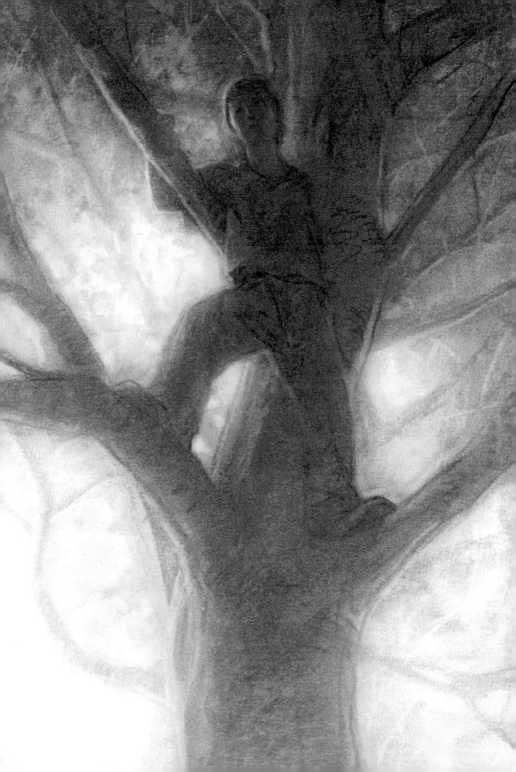

She got up, moving slowly. As she moved he did too, and before she reached the window he had disappeared. Completely. She looked down and he was nowhere to be seen.

Without thinking further, Kitty ran out of her room, down the wooden stairs and out of the front door. She sped round the side of the house and stopped. Nothing. It was as if he had never been there. She looked to the left across the lawn that rolled down towards the river. Nothing. Not even footprints in the slightly dewy grass. She looked right, down the driveway. Nothing.

She whistled for the dogs, thinking that it was very odd that they had not barked. They came running immediately, Annie out front on her fast whippety legs and Grouse not far behind her, looking for all the world as if he had just woken up.

Kitty shook her head. Perhaps she had imagined it all. A waking dream.

The more she thought about it, though, the stranger it became and, while she didn't like to admit to it, Kitty O'Brien started to feel just the beginnings of a knot of fear in her stomach and a small – a very small – shiver that ran down her back.

She breathed in. She would try and ignore it and go out to the field to fetch Chessie in. She pulled on a pair of old tracksuit pants over her pyjamas and grabbed her riding boots and the halter that was hanging near the back door.

Chessie was the easiest horse in the world to catch. As Kitty walked towards the gate she shook the scoop of nuts and Chessie lifted her head up, pricked her ears forward and set off at a fast trot up the field. She was at the gate before Kitty even reached it. Kitty slipped the halter on, buckled it up and started leading Chessie towards the lean-to shed where she kept her saddle. As they came closer to it, Chessie stopped suddenly and let out a most peculiar noise, half way between a whinny and a snort. She stamped her front hoof and shivered. Kitty looked at her: this was most unlike Chessie.

'Come on, girl,' she whispered, rubbing her hand down the side of the horse's neck, 'There's nothing here. And there's more food in the shed, you know that.'

But Chessie would not budge. She shook her head from side to side and planted her large hooves on the ground. Kitty might have been tall for her age but she was no match for a horse in this mood. She tried an old trick and started leading Chessie back the way they had come, in the hope that when they turned around Chessie might have forgotten why she'd stopped in the first place and then follow her. It didn't work. They were now even further away from the shed.

There are people who think that horses have brains the size of a butterfly, but they would be wrong. Chessie for one is a very clever creature. Something was troubling her and she had no intention of heading towards the source of that trouble. There was precious little Kitty could do about this and, as she didn't feel like spending the next hour persuading Chessie, she gave in and led her back to the field.

As she walked back towards the house, a flash of blue caught her eye, just next to the water trough. Only a flash – then it was gone. It looked very like the blue of the T-shirt that the boy had been wearing when he was standing at the top of the tree.

Kitty stopped, suddenly very aware of being alone, and as fast as she could she ran back into the house and upstairs to her bedroom. When she got inside, she slammed the window shut, locked the latch and then jumped into her bed and pulled the duvet over her head. She stayed that way, only the top of her hair uncovered, until her mum called her to come down for breakfast.

'You all right, sweetie?' her mum asked as Kitty came into the kitchen. 'You look terrible. You didn't go riding?'

Kitty shook her head. 'No, Chessie wouldn't go. She was frightened.'

'Chessie? She's never been frightened of anything!'

'Well, she was today. And I was as well, Mum,' Kitty said hesitantly, not knowing where to begin without sounding crazy.

'Of what?'

Kitty decided to tell the truth.

'You know the ash tree outside my window? Its branches were scratching on the glass this morning, and when I got up to look there was a boy standing on the tree. It was him moving the branch up and down.'

She looked up at her mum who was looking, to put it mildly, disbelieving.

'A boy?'

'Yes. He had a blue shirt on. He had straight black hair. I think he was Japanese.'

'Kitty, come on –' her mum started to say, then stopped. Her face paled and she stared at her daughter. 'Japanese?' she said quietly. 'Are you sure?'

'Yes, pretty sure,' Kitty said, starting to feel slightly shaky.

'How old was he?'

'I don't know, my age. Why, Mum, what's wrong?'

Her mother shook her head. 'Nothing at all, pet. Don't mind me; I didn't sleep well. I'm sure it was just a dream, Kitty. Don't worry about it at all. It's nothing.'

Kitty sat down at the table saying, 'It's not nothing. Even Chessie knew something was wrong.'

'The dogs didn't bark, did they?' her mum said, 'and you know they would if someone was here.'

'Well, I know, but still …'

'Forget all about it,' her mother said briskly, patting Kitty on her head. 'It never happened.'

It was just as well that at that point Kitty's other best friend, Sam, arrived, saving Kitty's mum from further explanations.

I will, however, tell you what happened as long as you promise to keep it a secret.

You see, in a house on Maudlin Street in the city, just a few miles along the river from Kitty's home, there'd lived a young boy called Akemi. His name, when translated into English, means Beautiful Dawn. He and his parents had moved from Tokyo to Kilkenny just a year before this.

Akemi's mother was a nervous soul and because of this she kept him close. She taught him at home and he was never allowed to stray far from the house. She promised him that one day he would go to school with other children but Akemi wasn't sure he believed her. It was a lonely life, and on summer evenings Akemi would look out of the top window of their home and watch the people walking along the pathway next to the River Nore. He loved the river and had read that it started up in the Devil's Bit mountain. One day, tired of being kept in the house, he decided he would try to make his way there.

At sunrise, before his mother and father woke up, he got out of bed, pulled on his favourite blue T-shirt and crept out of the back door. He walked along John's Quay, past Green's Bridge and finally onto the Bleach Road. This road winds with the river, and at the place where the road and the river touch there stands an old ash tree.

When Akemi reached the tree he looked up at it and took a fateful decision to climb it. Fateful because near the top of the tree the branches had already been weakened by the wild and wicked storms of 2012. Akemi was small for his age but strong and he climbed swiftly and easily up the tree. I am not going to go into details about what happened next – I will spare you that – but suffice to say that though the young boy felt no pain, from that day onwards he was no longer with us in human form.

It was a tragedy for his loving parents, for Akemi himself and, in some small way, for young Kitty O'Brien.

Kitty's mother, much like Akemi's mother, was very protective of her child. She had read in the newspaper of the sad death of the young Japanese boy from Maudlin Street but had never told Kitty, as she felt it would upset her, happening as it did so close to where they lived.

Who is to say whether she should have told her? I do not know. But Kitty never forgot the face of the young boy in the blue T-shirt. And Akemi himself, whose early-morning wanderings continued all through that summer, returned to her home just one more time. He etched a small message up in the top corner of Kitty's bedroom window.

'Beautiful horse' was all that it said.
Kitty hasn't found it yet, but one day she will.

Embedded in my Brain

by

SEAMUS CASHMAN

The whole world sits here, pointing to the stars.
Everywhere else sparkles in the dark and calls on me
to look down at my feet, grounded in a winter sea
in that once upon a time, and once upon a place
where I took a chance. I think it was a fishes' dance

that hurried up the shore waving adventure in my face.
There were songs of praise singing themselves
out there in the bay, and willing me to walk
from old Portmarnock beach to Malahide,
along those rocks that cuddle with the sea.

You'd think it easy, hop and leap, and leap
and hop from rock to rock there and back,
everyday stuff till daylight wakes; routine
all the way. But no, no, no! I slipped and fell.
Let out a yell. Ran back, crabbed out. I nearly died!

But a passing claw with a silver eye pinched my toe and winked.
I got the message, spun around and sang out loud,
O why go back if there's a front? Why sink
if there's a swim? Hop rocks and carry on.
Then, that squeaky voice – the winking crab again.

I heard it talk. I really did! A lyric now embedded in my brain:
Under water, under ground, we creep and crawl. We make our sounds:
We see touch, we hear pain. We taste the truth in every tale.
We're the water, we're the gravel, we're the rocks, seaweed and sand.
We're the ground that welcomes all. So – look around! Look around.

I looked – down at my feet and scratching there
at a bright white marbly stain, I saw a claw that disappeared.
I never used to listen to rock crabs,
or sand fleas on the beach, or seagull tribes or cormorants
carved upon the shore. But now my eager eyes were lasering

the ground. Curiosity pinched my nose. I hunkered down
to finger all those pimples on the rock. A million there or more.
The rock was cold but silk in parts, gentle to my touch. I wondered too
for other shapes were long, or wide, or prickly, pockmarked or map-like.
It 'welcomes all', that crab had said. Here perhaps is why:

this rocky shore is fossilised – this ground
is hardwired brain, all bumps and knobs and squelchy parts
– like yours or mine. It is an earth song in us all,
an ancient kin, an ancient call to dance and sing
beside a winter sea where you and I are we.

The
Ram
King

by

EOIN COLFER

The tiny kingdom of Exterios is based on Hook Head in Wexford where I spent every holiday moment as a child.

Once upon a place, which might be a far far away place depending on the distance this story has travelled, there was a very small kingdom called Exterios, which had been ruled by the Ram King for as long as anybody could remember. Exterios was an arrowhead peninsula bordered on two sides by a treacherous ocean, which was known by all the inhabitants of the kingdom as the Toodle-oo, because you could say toodle-oo to anyone who tried to cross it.

And it would come to pass that once in a blue moon a giant Battering Ram would survive the swim across the Toodle-oo and find his shaggy self driven salt-mad, with a craving for red meat. This was bad news for the Exteriors, as they were mostly composed of red meat, and so they would launch their coracles and bob on the Toodle-oo until the Battering Ram was bested in combat by that warrior who would become the next Ram King – or marry the current king's daughter.

Eventually the Battering Ram business stopped coming to pass, and by the time the reign of King Filan III came around, the battering rams were considered a myth and no-one really believed that the ram tales were based on anything more than the exaggerated account of some farmer's struggle to shear a moody sheep.

It was therefore both unfortunate and ironic that a Battering Ram showed up on Exterios during the annual Battering Ram Parade.

King Filan III was on the Ram Throne, which was pretty much like a wooden chair but with a ram's fleece draped over the high back, watching the Exterios Players re-enacting the famous legend of Filan I's defeat of the Great Dun Ram. Filan would have dearly loved to sneak off to his lodge for a snooze, but Queen Rosileen was visiting from the nearby kingdom of Salt Flats, and both sneaking and snoozing would have been considered very bad manners.

Not that Her Majesty would notice, thought Filan. *Old Rosileen can't see much beyond her nose without the aid of sand crystals.*

In the square, the players played with much banging of *bodhráns* and hard shoes on the planks and all was about as boring as it could get as far as Filan was concerned, when Queen Rosileen tapped his shoulder and said, 'Oh, Filan. That's very good. That's very realistic. That must have cost you a fortune.'

The phrase *cost you a fortune* penetrated the fog around Filan's brain and he sat upright on his throne and saw what was barging up the hill through the long meadow: a ram, larger than the grain storehouse, with corkscrew horns so big that a man could stand inside their span.

'Ram!' cried the king.

'Yes, Your Majesty,' said Scown, the baker. 'Isn't it wonderful?'

Filan jabbed a royal finger in the beast's direction.

'No, you fool. Battering Ram!'

Shortly after that, the screaming began.

The ram went through the village like a winter storm, stomping the houses to kindling, chewing the Exterios Players to pieces and tossing entire houses through the air. It was chaos.

Princess Aoibh jumped onto the Ram Throne, under which her father cowered, and shouted, in a very loud voice for a young lady, 'To the boats! Everybody make for the boats!'

No-one paid much attention, and Aoibh realised that she was using too many words for terrified people and so began to shout, 'Boats! Boats! Boats!' over and over until people got the message.

And so while the Battering Ram amused itself toying with the village's prize bull, the survivors snuck down to the village and boarded the coracles.

It was a long night for the Exteriors as they watched the destruction of their village. Eventually the ram knocked over a brazier and flames quickly spread through Exterios, until the entire hamlet resembled a hilltop beacon. The crackling flames made the giant ram sleepy, and it lay down in the fire's corona, its fleece glowing gold where the light caught its curls.

The first to speak was Queen Rosileen who was not in quite as much shock as the others.

'Honestly, Filan,' she said, 'this is the best re-enactment in years. A boat trip and everything.'

Some hours later the sun rose over a very weary, bleary bunch of Exteriors who could hardly believe that their past had come back to haunt them. The sun had barely cleared the horizon when all eyes turned to King Filan for guidance.

'What should we do, Your Majesty?' asked his subjects. 'Command us.'

Filan was not accustomed to making quick decisions under intense pressure. Or, for that matter, under any pressure.

'Commands,' he said. 'Yes, commands we must have.'

'What commands must we have, exactly?' asked his captain of the royal guards, of which there had been three, of which two were crushed and partially eaten.

Princess Aoibh took over. She stood on the coracle's cross-plank and cut an impressive figure, tall and flame-haired, with a wide intelligent brow and piercing green eyes.

'Good people,' she said. 'We cannot fight the ram, and we cannot remain here. Our only option is to row down the coast to the Kingdom of Salt Flats.'

Aoibh may have cut an impressive figure but the congregation were not impressed by this option.

'To brave the Toodle-oo means death!' cried a fisherman. 'Where the currents meet the headland they form whirlpools. We'd have to go many leagues out to deep waters to avoid the whirlpools, and in the depths the ocean would crush these little coracles.'

'And you are not drawing that creature to my kingdom,' said Queen Rosileen, who seemed very lucid all of a sudden.

'What other choice do we have?' asked Princess Aoibh.

The captain of the guard, whose name was Wulfus – which, it must be admitted, was an excellent name for a soldier – had a solution in mind.

'Your Majesty,' he called from two boats away, 'have you forgotten the Oration of Desperation?'

'Of course I haven't forgotten it, Wulfus,' snapped the king. 'The players were spouting it last night.'

'Allow me to quote a verse,' said Wulfus, eagerly, because as a boy he had dreamed of the day when he would single-handedly save the village from a Battering Ram. Nothing strange about that, but as an adult he had continued to dream about it, which was a little odd.

Wulfus cleared his throat and made quite a good fist of the Oration of Desperation:

Oh, who shall rid me of this hellish beastie,
I shall make him rich at leastie.
Take my crown to stop the slaughter
Or take the hand of my fair daughter.

Princes Aoibh was appalled. 'Please, Captain. This is not the stone age anymore. It's the iron age now. Nobody can pledge my hand.'

Wulfus shrugged. 'It's the law, beloved. And you will learn to love me in time.'

'Beloved?' spluttered Aoibh. It was her first public splutter, but she was quite flabbergasted. 'I hardly know you.'

'But *I* know *you*,' said Wulfus, which earned him a big *Awwwww* from the Exteriors, but which Aoibh thought was suspicious and creepy.

'And I have been practising,' continued Wulfus. 'With the Ramplements. In my private time, of course.'

This earned him a big *Ooooh* from the Exteriors, for the Ramplements were holy relics and were only supposed to be touched by the royal polisher with a goose feather.

King Filan rubbed his chin and said, 'Ummm.'

Aoibh could not believe it. 'Ummm?' she said. 'Ummm? Does that mean you are considering this?'

'I don't see any other option, Aoibh,' said her father.

'Then it's settled,' said Wulfus. 'If I can kill the ram, it's either Princess Aoibh's hand or the crown for me.' He winked at Aoibh. 'I think you can guess which one I will choose.'

And with those words, Captain Wulfus dived into the Toodle-oo and swam for the harbour.

Aoibh was torn between fury and disbelief. 'Father! How can you give me away, just like that, to a man I barely know?'

Filan swallowed. 'In time, my dear, you may come to love him.'

Princess Aoibh shook both fists and lunged, causing Filan to shriek and duck, but Aoibh was not attacking the king – she was after someone else. The princess's dive took her straight over the king's head and into the gentle summer wavelets of the Toodle-oo.

Filan was surprised. 'I didn't know Aoibh could swim,' he said.

But swim she could, and swim she did, gaining on Wulfus with every stroke.

Fortunately for this story's survival, Shenanigán, the village storyteller, who was a dead loss at physical labour but excellent at embellishment, had a clear view of the unfolding adventure, and realised that this was the moment all story-tellers dreamed about: to be the originator of an epic exploit.

I shall be the prime teller, he thought, and immediately began composing on the hoof. He dearly wished for some vellum and charcoal so he could scratch the small pictograms as the story unfolded, but he would have to store the words in his head for now. *There may be vellum a-plenty very soon.*

And these were the words composed in the mind of Shenanigán the storyteller:

And thus did begin the legend of the brave and noble Exterior, Captain Wulfus, who threw himself into the Toodle-oo, braving mountainous waves for the hand of his childhood sweetheart, the Princess Aoibh.

Wulfus swam for shore, seeing before him not the sheer Cliffs of Heartbreak, but the face of his dear Aoibh, for if he could but defeat the Battering Ram, then she would be for ever his.

Wulfus was mightily depleted on reaching the shore, but deter-mined to press on and scale the cliffs, when he heard a voice from the waters crying, 'Wulfus, oh my darling.'

And his heart beat like a battle drum, for it was none other than Aoibh in the water, splashing vainly in the chopping current, and so Wulfus lowered his mighty arms, lifted her clear of the cold Toodle-oo and laid her gently on a flat rock.

'Why have you come?' said he, distraught. 'There is danger here.'

And Aoibh kissed him and begged, 'Please, beloved, do not battle the ram. There must be another way.'

But there was no other path, not for a hero like Wulfus, for he was destined to save Exterios.

'Remain here,' he said to Aoibh, 'and presently I shall return for you.'

Such was Aoibh's love that she could not give her consent to the battle but simply turned her face aside.

Wulfus turned and sprang to grasp the cliff's lowest ledge.

He climbed until his hands were raw and bloodied. His only water came from the sky. Its price was a loss of sure footing, but Wulfus persevered until his boots were firmly planted on the long meadow. All around was devastation: flattened crops and devoured livestock, tumbled stone barns.

Wulfus knew he must retrieve the Ramplements from the king's lodge and so he ran in a hunched form along the long meadow, pausing only to roll his body in the offal of a cow which had been trodden upon by the ram. In this manner he hoped to mask the scent of the meat which the monster now had a taste for: the flesh of man.

Wulfus reached the town wall and it was there that fortune smiled on him not once but twice. For one, the ram, exhausted by its marauding, was sleeping atop the cooling ashes of a fire. And for two, the town wall had collapsed in many places, including the stretch which formed the rear wall of King Filan III's lodge, and so Wulfus simply stepped over the rubble and into the house; And there, on a vaulted plinth, rested the sacred Ramplements:

> The helmet of Filan I, which could withstand even the gnashing of the Battering Ram's enormous teeth
> The breastplate of Filan II which would protect the bones from any attempted goring
> The ramspear itself, which could never shatter and would pierce the toughest hide

Wulfus quickly donned the armour and hefted the spear, and not a moment too soon, for the ram had detected the scent of man.

In the village square, the Battering Ram's giant head shifted, leathery nostrils twitching. The ram snuffled, kicked out its back legs and, resting on its ancient horns, pushed itself upright.

The Exteriors cried and yelled, 'Run, brave Wulfus! Flee.' For they were certain he could not prevail against such a beast, but the Toodle-oo snatched away their pleas.

The ram sniffed out his breakfast and thundered across the village and, perhaps because it somehow suspected that there might be a threat waiting behind the lodge door, the monster reared up on its powerful hind legs and leaped high, over the wall lodge, and butted downwards through the thatched roof.

The watchers could see no more, for both ram and captain were lost in a haze of dust, straw, stone and splinter. There was great commotion, mighty thrashings and stompings and entire sections were blown out as though by combustion.

Shenanigán knew that he was waffling, but he couldn't make out any details. *I shall ask Wulfus for those details,* he decided. *If he survives.*

It did not look good for Wulfus, it had to be said, for moments later the mighty ram shrugged off the lodge as though it were an ill-fitting coat, and pranced back towards the warm ashes, not seeming in the least injured.

Oh dear, thought Shenanigán. *I'd best compose a tragic ending.*

It seemed as though the valiant Wulfus had given his life for love. The ram, sated by the blood and bone of Exterios's hero cleaned its hoofs on the upturned throne and then settled once more onto the fire's cooling ashes to warm his belly.

Oh, devil.

Oh, foul monster.

You have broken the princess's heart. You have broken all our hearts and dashed our dreams on the Cliffs of Heartbreak.

But wait. But lo.

The ram was in some discomfort. It thrashed and bucked and sought to rise but could not find traction. It threw back its mighty head and screamed in pain.

Injured it was, there could be no doubt.

Could it be that Wulfus had struck a blow before he died?

The ram's bleating screams grew louder, echoing across the black water to Exterior ears. Again and again the ram attempted to rise, but whatever injury afflicted the beast had robbed it of strength and it was all it could do to roll from its bed of ashes, leaving behind a pile of glistening organs and a lake of blood hissing on the ash.

And from within the organs came a movement. The heart perhaps? Still beating?

But no, for the movement became a thrust, and from the pyramid of organs emerged the figure of a warrior clad in and bearing the Ramplements.

Wulfus lived. Praise the gods! The hero has conquered. Swallowed in the belly of the beast and yet with the fortitude to strike from the inside!

As though feeling the eyes of the Exteriors upon him, Wulfus raised his spear in triumph.

The ram was dead.

Exterios was saved.

The coracles were rowed to harbour across a flat, calm sea just in time to meet the hero of the hour as he strolled down the gentle slipway.

'Good Wulfus,' cried King Filan, 'you have saved us. I would pay a thousand daughters for your service.'

The hero pulled off the helmet to reveal Princess Aoibh underneath.

'Really, father? A thousand daughters?'

Confusion reigned.

Aoibh?

Princess Aoibh was the ram warrior?

'Ummm,' said Filan.

'Where is the captain?' asked Queen Rosileen. 'Perished?'

Aoibh scooped ram gore from her neck. 'Perished? No, Captain Eternal Love got a cramp in the ocean. I had to save his old carcass and then kill the ram.'

This was simply astounding talk. Unprecedented.

'Ummm,' began her father. Then: 'But how? How, my dear? Did the beast swallow you?'

Aoibh was flabbergasted. 'Swallow me, father? How could you think that? I am uninjured. The ram slept on the warm ashes, so after the lodge collapsed I buried myself in the ashes. Then I –'

Aoibh made a stabbing motion, straight up.

'Yes, I see,' said the king. 'That makes a lot more sense than being swallowed alive.'

'I used to practise with the Ramplements too,' said Aoibh.

Aoibh walked down the slipway till she was waist-deep in the Toodle-oo, so that the ram's blood could be sluiced away from her trunk.

'And now, father, my reward.'

Filan flapped his hands. 'Reward? You can hardly take your own hand in marriage.'

'Very well,' said Princess Aoibh. 'Then I shall have the crown.'

'Ummm,' said Filan. 'Perhaps you could take your own hand. But what does that mean?'

Princess Aoibh emerged from the salt water and unbuckled the breastplate. 'It means that I shall marry the man I want to marry without any interference from you, father.'

King Filan was about to protest, but he felt the weight of his crown upon his head and decided he would like to keep it there.

'Very well. You may marry a man of your choosing.'

'If a suitable man comes along.'

'If a suitable man comes along.'

As it happened, a suitable man had already come along, but Aoibh did not notice him for many years, and by the time Scown the baker delivered her feast-day brack she was already queen of Exterios. Scown won the Queen's heart with a witty series of pictograms which read: *Hail, Queen Aoibh, she will pierce your heart.*

Aoibh smiled when she read her feast-day message and said: 'Good Master Scown. Sit beside me and break bread.'

Scown was happy to oblige.

Snail
Pals

by

GERALDINE MILLS

I hear Lia calling
   as the sun high-fives the sky.
I look out the window of my whorly, twurly house,
   and there we are nose to eye.

She lifts me up from behind tall grass,
   rests me in her palm.
'No lolling around in your PJs, today,'
   she's as bossy as my snaily mam.

Along the rumbly road we go,
   I snail jog along beside her.
She tells me about her favourite place:
   the castle at Aughnanure.

When my slim-slimy foot is nearly kaput,
    we arrive at the field of yews.
The Drimneen river gurgles about
    deep caverns and swirly pools.

She leads me up to the turret top
    with its ancient, spirally stair.
Big white clouds puff around my horns
    so cold, I wish I had hair.

From this spot we see Lough Corrib,
    a fisherman in his boat.
The Twelve Bens so tall, they tickle the sky,
    below us the foaming moat.

She tells of the ferocious O'Flahertys
    who ruled the whole place once.
How the Tribes within the city walls
    quaked at their savage stunts.

She shows me the lookout tower,
    its secret, vaulted room.
The murder hole that a guest never guessed
    till he plopped to his watery tomb.

Now here we sit at the top of the world,
    lord and lady of all we survey.
And we dine on greens and yum jelly beans,
    BFFs in all of Galway.

Number

13

by

JIM SHERIDAN

Johnny carries a monster on his back.

The monster is only a boy, but he's been on Johnny's back for fifty years now.

When Johnny looks in the mirror he sees the monster boy peeping over his shoulder and tells him that he could never live without him. This keeps the boy happy. When Johnny goes to bed, the boy sits on the ground keeping watch while Johnny sleeps.

You're a great minder, Johnny tells him, but the boy doesn't fall for compliments.

If he is really fed up with Johnny, the boy climbs the walls really fast, which is his way of letting Johnny know that he is *driving him up the walls*. The boy could just say the words but he prefers to act things out sometimes.

If Johnny takes too much strong drink in the pub, then the boy walks along the bar counter to glare at him. This is to let Johnny know he should go to the toilet. The boy behaves properly in the toilet and turns his head away when Johnny is going. And if Johnny has to use the stall for a

number two, then the boy leaves him alone, but all the time his feet are visible under the door to let Johnny know he is still there. After a few minutes the boy bangs the door once only to make sure Johnny flushes, and by the time Johnny comes out the tap is already running. The boy makes sure that Johnny washes his hands the way a doctor does: back and front and in between the fingers. Then the boy shows Johnny how to wash his thumb, holding it with his full hand and turning it, like the way you start up a motorbike.

Johnny never took a wife because the boy would not hear of it. Johnny is seventy now and works for a fair, travelling around the country because the boy would not have it any other way. The boy makes all the decisions for them both.

The boy first jumped on Johnny's back fifty years ago because Johnny had gone into the boy's house.

Number 13.

Johnny used to live in Number 13 himself, and he wanted to see if it had the same feel as it had when he was young. When he tried to explain this to the boy, telling him the term for this was *a sense of place*, the boy said that this was stupid, and senseless terms were just a way for the grown-ups to get on your back.

Get off my back, the boy shouted so many times that tears came to his eyes.

When Johnny entered Number 13, all those years ago, at first he couldn't feel anything because of course they had changed the wallpaper and drawers. Johnny felt that they should have asked his permission to make changes even though all the old stuff was wrecked.

Number 13 was all fixed up after the fire and for sale again, so Johnny had gone there pretending that he was going to buy it. He lied to the man selling it, telling him that he really loved the house but wanted to stay there for a few minutes on his own so he could get a feel for it.

When the man left, Johnny closed his eyes and felt his way along the walls. He walked into the bathroom and tried to remember what it was like when he lived there but he couldn't, so he locked the door and peed into the toilet. When some pee splashed on the seat, Johnny remembered that these splashes used to drive his dad mad.

Dad mad.

Mad dad.

Dad dead.

Johnny closed his eyes once more and then walked his hands along the walls, through the house, until they found the back door. He felt the lock and opened the door and then went into the yard all in blackness.

A cow had run into the yard once. A cow, in the middle of Dublin!

It came for tea, his mam said.

His dad said they were taking it to Liverpool for it to be meat instead of a cow: Sirloin, fillet and hooves. But no-one could eat the cow's feet.

And it was a smart cow trying to get away.

Johnny's dad was funny, but it was his mammy who ran the cow out the back door.

She came back in, walking like a country woman. This was a side of her Johnny had never seen before, and he asked her to do the country walk again, but she just rubbed his head and smiled.

And now, when Johnny closed his eyes and felt the concrete yard under his feet, he could feel her hand there on his head.

Johnny knew the hand was not really there because he was not a thick like the teachers told him. He did not even believe that his mother had a hand any more. After she died, the maggots got the hands after they ate the steak parts. The sirloin parts.

But no-one could eat a cow's feet, his dad had told him. They made sure of that. Smart they are.

Johnny does not believe his mam is in heaven.

What would she do all day?

Walk around with the cows?

No. If it was true that you could do whatever you wanted in heaven, then his mammy would really come back and make tea in the house for him. So there must not be a heaven.

After the yard, Johnny felt his way back into the kitchen and he imagined himself going to all the drawers that used to be there, and opening them and looking at the pictures of his mam and dad who were dead. In his photographs his parents opened their eyes and winked at him. First Johnny thought they were telling him, *Yes, we are dead. So no heaven, OK?*

But Johnny's mammy and daddy were not winking at him about heaven. They were trying to tell him something else. Something about love. Johnny could only ever read love in his mam's eyes, so everything she did had a smile in it.

Johnny walked up the stairs and he knew there were twenty-two exactly and that they all measured five inches, so the total was a hundred and ten inches, which was like two little Johnnies on top of one another. When Johnny got to the top step, he put his hand out to open the child-proof gate. And even though the gate was not there he still opened it in his mind. It even squeaked like it had in the old days because *some bad boy had not put oil on the gate had he?*

Some bad boy had not locked the gate one night.

The squeak woke the boy. And he jumped on Johnny's back. Johnny opened his eyes but of course he could not see the boy because he was on his back, so Johnny twisted round and round trying to get him off.

Then he realised the boy had hands.

Small hands.

He tried to beat them off.

He even tried to bite them, but it was no use. After all, everybody knows you can't hurt monsters like that boy. Johnny closed his eyes and then opened them but the hands were still there. He closed his eyes for a long time like when a car won't start and you have to give it time, like his dad used to say. When he opened them the hands were still there. This time he closed his eyes and said a prayer.

To God.

But God laughed.

Johnny really heard God laughing.

Ha ha ha ha ha ha.

God had tears in his eyes from the laughing.

Johnny closed his eyes and thought about asking the devil for help, but things were bad enough without the top man on the other side coming into it. And that top man could not beat the other top man. Everybody knew that from school.

So Johnny closed his eyes and asked his mother for help.

Mam, Mam, Mam, Mam, Mam, came out of his mouth like it used to when he was walking down the road after she died.

But he opened his eyes and the hands were still there. His mammy couldn't help him.

Johnny closed his eyes one more time and tried to think of nothing. But that's impossible.

When he had the eyes closed not thinking of nothing, he heard a boy's voice say *Look, no hands,* like when you drive a car, if you're mad.

He opened his eyes again and saw the boy was a monster. Johnny tried to shake the boy off but he would not budge. The boy had the two legs around Johnny like he was a rodeo rider and Johnny was a bucking bronco.

Johnny decided to run into the wall. He smacked the boy off the wall but it was Johnny who felt the pain in his head like a piece of coal that burned bright. So bright that Johnny was blind again but this time with his eyes open.

The boy clasped his hands around Johnny's neck, and Johnny remembered that his favourite thing in this life was jockey-backs from his dad. Not as good as ice-cream, but now that he can't eat ice-cream anymore with the pain in his teeth the jockey-backs take first place.

The boy held onto Johnny good and tight and did not climb down for three whole weeks and by that time Johnny knew that the monster-boy was with him for life. Or until one of them died.

And all because of what had happened.

From then on the boy made all the decisions. They ate what he liked to eat. All kids' stuff like chips and battered sausages, which gave Johnny a big belly like a woman who was expecting. And they slept where the boy wanted which was in tents or forts in the woods or a sleeping bag on a fine night. The boy made Johnny swim too, no matter how freezing cold the sea was, because monsters don't feel cold – everybody knows that.

They say life is short, but for Johnny it went on for an eternity, always living a boy's life, so no girls or books. Plenty of fighting, though, and chasing dogs. That was the boy's favourite.

And no stupid indoor jobs. That was top of the list. So Johnny ended up doing whatever needed to be done at the fair. They called him the world's oldest stable-boy.

Johnny was mopping out a carriage in the ghost train one night when the boy made him an offer.

'I'm going to give you a chance, John,' he said, and his accent was Dublin like Johnny's own. 'If you can answer three questions.'

Johnny was so surprised that all he could do was nod.

'Question one,' said the boy. 'Do you know who I am?'

Of course Johnny knew. He wasn't a thick, no matter what those teachers had said all those years ago.

'Yeah,' he said, finding his voice. 'I know all right.'

The boy seemed pleased. 'And do you know why I decide everything?'

Johnny knew this one as well. He'd had fifty years to think about it. Most nights he dreamed about it too.

'You decide now, because I decided to leave the gate open in case it would squeak when I snuck out. Then you got downstairs and the fire and all. Sure you were only a young fella.'

This made the boy cross. 'So I decide. And we do what I like. What I would have done.'

'If I hadn't left the gate open.'

'Yeah. You and your sneaking out. Girls are nothing but trouble.'

The boy held up three fingers. 'Now. The hard question. Would you like me to leave you alone?'

Johnny thought this must be a trick.

Leave him alone? After all this time? To sleep in a bed or eat some vegetables or take a wash for himself whenever he felt like it.

'Alone?' was all he could say. 'Alone?'

The boy climbed into the front carriage of the ghost train. The one shaped like a skull. 'Alone,' he said.

And off the train went, though no-one had pressed the start button, and the boy disappeared into the tunnel whooping and screaming like a real live child might, and Johnny just watched him go, and then stood staring at the black mouth of the tunnel.

Was he alone now?

The train took eight and a half minutes to complete its circuit and when it emerged onto the platform once more, Johnny was still standing there with the mop in his hand and the bucket of slops between his feet.

'You couldn't decide, could you, John?' said the boy, climbing out of the skull carriage.

'No,' said Johnny. 'I can't decide because I left the gate open. It's better if you decide.'

The boy nodded, and Johnny knew he would never get such an offer again.

When Johnny had finished mopping out the ghost train, he hunched down so the boy could climb on his back, and he gave him a jockey-back to the stables where they were sleeping in a canvas tent rigged up in an empty stall.

There
and
Here

by **JANE MITCHELL**

My brother Benjamin thinks he knows everything. Because he's a boy. Because he's older than me. And because he always has his nose stuck in a book.

'The name *Phoenix* comes from Greek mythology,' he says. 'It is the bird of fire that rose from the ashes.'

Except this time I know he's wrong.

'It comes from *fionn uisce*,' I tell him. 'That means "clear water" in Irish.'

Benjamin doesn't like being wrong. He's the oldest son and always has to be right. Especially since Papa put him in charge.

'Until I arrive in Ireland with your brothers,' Papa had said to Benjamin at the airport, 'you must mind your sisters and your mama. You are the man now. That is why I am sending you.'

When we said goodbye to Papa and my little brothers, Benjamin was the only one who stayed strong and kept his crying on the inside. I think he was practising at being a man.

To me, Papa said: 'And you mind your tongue, Tanza.' This was nothing new. Papa was always telling me to mind my tongue: 'A smart tongue is never good for a girl. It will get you in trouble. No man wants to marry a smart girl.'

'Maybe I don't want to marry,' I told him.

'Listen to what Benjamin tells you,' Papa said. And to Mama: 'It is safer to get you and the girls out first.'

He was right but I still lie awake at night and worry about them. The boys are so small and Papa has to work long hours to get the money to travel. Even though she is awake too, Mama doesn't like to talk about it.

'Worrying does not help anyone,' she says. 'There is nothing we can do.'

'Who told you it means "clear water"?' Benjamin asks me now.

'My teacher,' I said. 'She said Phoenix Park is the biggest enclosed park in Europe.'

My teacher also told me that girls can go to college in Ireland if they want. And they can get jobs without the permission of their fathers or brothers. But I don't tell Benjamin this.

'You should never go alone to the park, Tanza,' he says. 'Even if it is the biggest enclosed park in Europe. It is not proper for a girl to be on her own. You must come straight home after school.'

I look around the room in the centre where we live. There is the bed I share with Mama and baby Gracie. There is the mattress on the floor where Benjamin sleeps. There are the plastic bins they gave us to keep our clothes in. The window is nailed shut and the bathroom is down the hall, shared with five other families. Even in my home country, we did not have to share our toilet place with five families, but in Ireland, we are not free to find our own home. We might even be sent back to my home country.

'This room is not my home,' I say to Benjamin. 'This centre is not my home.'

'It is home, Tanza,' Benjamin says, 'until Papa arrives with the boys. Then we will find a new place to live.'

The centre is full of strangers speaking in foreign languages who have also left people behind. Nights are haunted with broken dreams and broken families. In the daytime, people pace the halls like lost ghosts. We wait in queues for the toilet, hopping from foot to foot, and in the canteen for strange foods that I have never seen before. Mama has not been allowed to cook since we got here.

'How will you learn to prepare traditional dishes?' she says as she oils and braids my hair. She has taken to oiling and braiding my hair every night even though it doesn't need it. 'You will only know these Irish foods. Burgers and chips and beans. These are not the dishes of our people.'

When Mama thinks about us only eating Irish food, she jerks the threads in my braids way too tight.

'But I will know how to braid hair,' I tell her as I push her fretting hands away.

We have been living in this room for too long now. When we arrived, Gracie was a curled little thing always on Mama's breast. Now she has stretched out her bones and filled her skin. Sweet and round as a mango, she holds my hand and toddles

next
to me as we
walk the halls of
the centre. Papa won't
recognise her.

I don't tell my school friends
I live in one room with my family.
Benjamin doesn't tell his school friends
either. I see him in the yard at break-time,
sitting on his own, reading his book.

I don't go back to the centre after school.
Instead, I sneak into Phoenix Park like Benjamin told
me not to. He is not my papa. He is not in charge of
me. I go through the gate across from my school and walk
up the main avenue. The grassy fields open out on each side
under a big sky that reminds me of the sky in my home
country. I see the friendly grove where the trees hold hands
overhead. I push my way through the bushes to lie under
those trees and I breathe the green air. A thousand leaf-cuts
of sun make lace on my skin. Cool grass is soft beneath me.

We don't have green air in my home country. We don't
have leaf-cuts of sun in my home country. We don't have
soft green grass in my home country. In my home country,

the
sunshine is
loud and hard and
heavy. It sucks up the
green air and leaves behind
dust storms and heat-shimmer
and brown earth. But Phoenix Park
makes magic in my heart. There is
nobody here to laugh at my mixed-up
English. Nobody here to stare at my threaded
hair. To turn away from my foreign smell. Here in
the Park, the earth seeps its dark goodness into my
bones and fills me. My blood sings and I feel no shame.

Then I hear it. A movement in the bushes behind the
trees. I stiffen and lift my head. I turn all my hearing to the
sound, give over my whole body to listening. Branches
shake. Shadows flicker. I rise up on my elbows. Have the
boys from my class followed me here? Perhaps even the
bigger boys from Benjamin's class? When I see a leg push
through the bushes, I reach for my bag. If I have to run, I
don't want to leave my school books behind.

The leg is followed by an arm. Then a second arm that
pushes and reaches for branches. This person is slow as a

dung beetle. I recognise the school uniform: the same as mine. It is a boy and he has his head down. Not that it matters because I don't need to see his face. I know his movements. I know his long legs. I know the set of his shoulders. It is my brother Benjamin. He has followed me here.

My heart races and my scalp tingles. I want to grab my schoolbag and run but I can't move. All I can do is shrink small as an ant and worry what he will say to me. I know how angry he can get. I stay still as a mantis and hope that the fluttering leaf-lace hides me in its shadows.

But Benjamin is looking neither for me nor at me. He doesn't even see me. He throws his schoolbag on the ground. He drops to the grass, leans his elbows on his knees and holds his head in his hands. I think for a moment that he is praying, but this isn't any prayer position I know. He stays still, like he is thinking deeply. I stay still too, to watch him. What is this? He doesn't look like the almost-man that he is back at the centre.

He doesn't look bossy and in charge: the boy who knows everything. He looks tired. He looks a little bit lost. But what can I do? In my home country, a girl doesn't go near a troubled boy, even if he is her brother. Boys and men meet to chew leaves and talk; girls and women meet to wash clothes and talk. But we are no longer in my home country; there are no men or boys for Benjamin to talk to. My heart beats hard in my chest. I should sneak away, but I also want to talk to Benjamin, even though he will be so angry to see me here.

I crouch on my hunkers, but before I can stir, something startles Benjamin. Maybe the green air breathed on him. Maybe the lace shadows trembled. He whips his head up. He fixes his eyes on me like a snake about to strike.

'Tanza!' His voice is loud and sharp as a slap. 'You dare to sneak up on me in my hiding place? To stick your nose into my business?'

His hiding place? I was here first.

'I didn't sneak up on you,' I tell him. 'I came here on my own. This is *my* hiding place.'

As soon as the words are out of my mouth, I remember too late Papa's warning about my smart tongue getting me into trouble.

'I told you to go straight back to the centre.' Benjamin's voice flashes like a new blade. His cheeks are bright and his eyes have fire in them, but I also see dark currents running deep. 'You disobeyed me.'

This is not fair, even if he is in charge.

'*You* didn't go back to the centre,' I say. 'You are here also.'

'It is different,' Benjamin says. 'You are a girl. You should be at home.'

'It is not different.' I cannot hide the indignation spiking my voice. 'That centre is not home. There is nothing like home about it. Papa is not there. The boys are not there. Mama is not allowed to cook. And you've turned bossy.'

Benjamin says nothing at first. He might explode because of my backchat. But when he speaks, the blaze has burned out of his voice.

'You are right,' he says. 'That centre is no home. It doesn't smell like home. It doesn't feel like home. And burgers, chips and beans certainly don't taste like home.'

I stare at Benjamin and, for once, I am wise enough to say nothing. He breathes out. He looks down at the grass.

'I am the man of our family,' he says. 'But I do not feel like a man, Tanza.' His voice is soft. 'It is difficult to be a man in a new country where everything is different and strange.'

'Do you remember back home, Benjamin, when Mama sent us to buy teff?' I say. Benjamin looks at me.

'We stopped for a break at the corn stall,' I tell him.

Benjamin's eyes brighten with interest. He remembers. 'We bought a cob each. We ate them sitting on the bank overlooking the fields.'

I nod, smiling, as the old Benjamin peeks from inside the new Benjamin.

'Here in this park, in this grove of trees,' I say, 'we can take a short break from this new life. You can take a break from being a man. You can be a boy here. There is no shame in that.'

Benjamin looks at me as he thinks about what I said. 'And what about you? What will you take a break from?'

I lie back on the soft green grass and let Phoenix Park work its magic on me. I breathe the green air.

'I will take a break from listening to you bossing me all the time,' I say.

Benjamin laughs. It is the first time I have heard my brother laugh in a long time.

'Maybe having a smart tongue is not so bad after all,' he says.

The Dirty River, Stillorgan

by

MARK GRANIER

Under the ivy-saddled stone
walls of St. John of God's asylum,
time slowed to a trickle: our own
mucky stretch of the Amazon.

Here I come, ready or not

Dirty River. The name stuck:
little more than a stream that still
mutters and gutters, deeply tucked
into the trees and foaming bramble.

Here I come, ready or not

Steep-banked, slippery, nettles and moss,
a whiff of sewage when rains swell
and hurry it, somewhere to go get lost,
space they couldn't develop or sell.

Here I come, ready or not

Somewhere to run when we got kicked
out of doors into afternoons
of Kick-the-Can and Hide-and-Seek,
of hold-your-breath and screech-balloons.

Here I come, ready or not

Chuckling out of a concrete pipe,
deep-shadowed, barely showing its face
before scuttling into the echoey, ripe
darkness below the new housing estates.

Here I come, ready or not

A river, a room, an alley – you make
your own clearing or find a niche
lit from within, an underground lake
rippling with each secret wish –

Ready or not, there you come

Stream
Time

by

OISÍN MCGANN

So there I am, floating down a river in a small leaky boat with no paddle and only my own corpse for company. It is a shock, I can tell you, to find yourself in a confined space with a dead body. It is worse to see that body wearing your own face.

Can you wake up to realise you're dead? Well, that's how it was. I woke up and found myself deceased. I opened my eyes as if I had only just closed them for an instant, and found myself sitting at the front of a boat, with no idea how I'd got there. Looking around, I saw only water, shrouded by a thick fog. The boat was moving on a gentle current, but I didn't know where. Water sloshed around in the bottom of the boat. I looked behind me.

It took me a moment to understand that the person behind me was dead, lying on her back, her head pointed towards me. It was another, longer moment peering at the upside-down face before I realised who it was.

And I would surely have toppled overboard in fright, if it wasn't for the water. For it might be a scary thing to see your own dead body, but it's nothing to how I feel about water. It puts the fear of God in me.

When I was *alive*, it was plain old *drowning* that used to scare me. We lived in a small village by the Boann river, and when I was a youngster, playing by the water, I slipped on a wet rock and fell into a deep part of the river. My mother pulled me out in time, scolding me for giving her such a scare, but I still have nightmares of sinking down through that dark, muddy gloom, choking on water, screaming bubbles.

Now that I've passed on, it is no longer drowning that bothers me. For it seems that ghosts don't drown.

When I first saw my dead body in the boat, I jerked backwards. One hand caught the top edge of the boat, and I managed to stop myself falling in, the small craft rocking violently. But my other hand slipped on the slimy wood and plunged down into the water. When I pulled it back out, it was gone. My hand was gone. Everything from halfway down my left forearm was gone. My first thought was that something in the water had bitten it off, but surely I would have felt that. And, though I was in a state of utter shock, I was in no pain. There was no blood. It was more like that part of me had *dissolved* in the water.

I had a good old scream, right then. Screaming as loud and as long as I did should have robbed me of my breath and even hurt my throat, but it seems that's another thing about being a ghost.

You've air a-plenty and you can keep letting it out for as long as you like.

Having got that out of me, I calmed down and stared at my arm. It was then that I realised something had changed in my head. I *knew* more. Looking around, I could see that the fog was clearing. I knew where I was. I was on the Boann, somewhere west of Baile Átha Troim – also known, as I somehow seem to know, as Trim.

Because that's another thing that has happened. I'm using words now that I've never spoken in my life. The name of the river has changed; you would call it the 'Boyne'. Up until the point where I lost my left hand, I had never been able to speak English. We had little need of it, for we hardly saw a single foreigner from one year to the next. All trade was in our native Irish.

As well as this new gift for language, I can now sense the lives of others around me. Floating down the river, passing the towering oak trees and the grassy banks, I can sense the minds of the living near by like a bee can find flowers. This new sense is how I know that *you're* there now. Yes, *you*. I can feel you looking into my head, listening to me. This language I'm using is *yours*, not mine, and it is a strange thing altogether.

I look at where my left hand used to be. I have gained this new knowledge, but it has cost me a part of myself. Now I'm even more scared of the water, for I think it is made up of souls, of ghosts and their memories, and I am terrified that they want to pull me in to join them. They can go and hang!

The banks either side are much too far away for my liking and, though I thought I was familiar with this part of the river, it seems different. There aren't so many trees and I can see the shapes of houses that were not there before. The buildings are different too. The roofs are still thatched, but more of them are rectangular, made of turf or even stone instead of the round post-and-wattle dwellings I know. How could things have changed so quickly?

As this thought crosses my mind, I remember the water in the bottom of the boat. It is a few inches higher than it was. I yelp like a puppy when I see my toes are gone, where the blasted water was lapping up against them. There can be no doubt about it: this boat is sinking. A chill runs through me and I shiver, pulling my feet back up onto the wooden board that serves as a seat.

Don't ask me what kind of boat it is. A wooden one, with *no paddles*, or oars or what have you – that much I can say. It's about twice the length of my body, which is lying on a deep bed of thin branches. As I take this in, I realise how I ended up here. The illness that had me coughing up my guts for weeks had done for me in the end. As for the *boat*, well I bet I have my misty-eyed, drunken sot of a husband to thank for that. Wasn't he always going on about his Viking heritage and how he would have been a chieftain or a king or some-thing if only his great-great-grandfather had stayed back in the Norse country? What senseless rot that man could talk! And Viking funerals were the only ones worth having, he used to say.

So he must have tried to give me one of those, the fool. He and my son together, no doubt, put me on this decaying, leaking boat, set fire to the branches beneath my body and pushed me out into the river. Those branches would just have been starting to catch, to make for a lovely funeral pyre out on the water. Oh, I'm sure it would have been a *grand* sight.

Except neither of them could ever light a fire to save their lives, especially not with the damp soaking through the bottom of this wretched tub. What kind of madman even goes out on the water in such a small craft anyhow? Sure I've seen *shoes* bigger than this boat.

And never mind that I'm a Christian, not one of those Norse pagans – or at least that's what I'll tell God if I see him. I was never the praying type. My life is – *was* – hard enough that I didn't have much time to be thanking God or anyone else for it. We had a decent plot of land, good rich soil, but the farm was small for our needs and it was hard to get enough out of it to keep us fed.

I'm worried now that this botched funeral has spoiled my chances of finding a place for my soul to land, now that I'm a ghost, as I seem to be. How am I to get off this damned river? A funeral pyre on a leaky boat! Lord preserve us from the good intentions of idiots.

There is definitely something different about the land. As I drift towards Trim, I can see a mysterious stone tower over the trees ahead of me. Rounding a long bend, I am astonished by the sight of a high stone wall around the town. As if that is not enough, the tower juts above it.

It seems it's just one part of an arching building with large windows, formed of stones so smooth and shaped as to be fit for God himself. But no sooner have I set eyes on that then I pass a copse of alder trees on my right and I am stunned by the spectacle of a castle that dwarfs the first building.

I cannot understand what I am seeing. I have visited Trim for the market on a few occasions. The town as I knew it was a bustling place, surrounded by defences of earth and wood, made up of humble buildings, not like the grandeur I'm seeing now. The people I see now are wearing strange clothes, with colours I have never seen in a fabric. They seem unaware of me, though every now and then a child points at me, crying, or a dog barks frantically. Otherwise, I am a ghost, passing by unseen.

As the river carries me on, under an arching stone bridge, I gaze down at the stump of my left forearm, lost in thought, bewildered, tears running down my cheeks. For a long time, I keep my head down, unwilling to see more of this changed landscape. I can't make head or tail of it and it has shaken my heart. I look up and catch a glimpse, far to my right, of the Hill of Tara, home of the High King. Then the river bends to the left, taking me away to the north. The current quickens. Rocks beneath the surface are whipping the water into a white froth, tossing the boat about. I grip the edge in sick fear with my one remaining hand.

Here and there on the banks, I see more people. Each man, woman or child that I see has the look of one who is starving. There is a famine here, poverty – and yet the buildings I am sweeping towards are not hovels, but solid constructions of small, evenly shaped bricks. This is some kind of town. Many of these buildings look tired and worn already, though they have tiled roofs and glass in the windows.

My new knowledge is failing me now, but this is a mystery I cannot bear to let pass. Gritting my teeth, I lean over and dip just the tip of my left arm in the water. I lose a couple of inches more and fresh awareness floods my mind. Yes, a famine, the like of which the country has never seen. We are servants of the English now, the poor in the countryside reduced to surviving on the potato – and that crop has failed. They come to the towns in the hope of work. I am in Navan, An Uaimh, though I could never have believed it. People have the look of the dead about them. And yet, I notice, they still can't see *me*.

As if by magic, a bridge is assembling across the river in front of me, the builders moving like flickering insects, the tall arches spanning giant stone legs. Here is proof that time is passing me at speed: I glimpse frozen moments and then they are gone. The flow of the river takes me under one of the bridge's arches and onwards.

Something huge and powerful gives a whistling howl as it thunders across the bridge above and behind me. I flinch and cower in terror, arms over my head. But then I turn to look. Whatever it was is gone, trailing a cloud of smoke. The Boyne is joined by another river, the Blackwater, as I turn sharply east. The trees have all but disappeared from the landscape.

Small woodlands stand where there should have been forests. What have they done with all the trees?

It is not long before I reach Baile Shláine – Slane.

I have never been here before. Its round hills rise up on either side of me. There is another castle to my left, much smaller and newer than Trim's. The air has a strange smell, dank with smoke. Has there been some great war? The water in the boat is several inches deep now, and the decrepit craft is moving heavily, sluggishly. I dip a heel cautiously into the cold liquid and learn more.

There are *machines* now. Steel monsters that consume coal. They are spewing smoke like dragons. The taste of it is in the air. The Boyne carries me towards Drogheda, Droichead Átha, and the sky is shrouded in smog. The cloud of darkness gradually clears ahead of me and the air grows cleaner. Another bridge, this one built from white, seamless stone and taut cables, impossibly delicate, suddenly fills the sky above me. I gasp, arching my neck to gaze up at it. The world feels warmer, more humid now, as I approach the town. The river bulges against its banks, flooding fields. I float past a strange assortment of buildings from different centuries. One old fort, high on a hill to my right, looks like a cup in a bowl. What a strange, mixed-up place this world has become! It is beautiful and perplexing and overwhelming all at once.

My rotten, floundering boat is dwarfed by giant ships of steel, built for conquering oceans. The river swells high up on the stone walls that hem it in on either side. Another bridge, towering on ageing pillars, forms a gateway to the stretch I know will take me to the sea.

I have been rigid with
fear on this river for so long, seen so
much. All that lies ahead of me is the deep sea and I feel a
sense of horror at its vast emptiness. Then I realise my feet
have dissolved and, to my surprise, the tension begins to lift
from me. Finally, I understand that no ghost is meant to wait
this long. It is not my fate to haunt a sinking boat. I am desperately lonely: I miss my husband's rough laugh, the crush
of my son's hugs. I am sorry to leave them, but I must.

The boat is still struggling to stay afloat. I can see the mouth of the river now, opening to the sea. It is time. It has been time all along. Rolling gently out of the boat, I let myself slip into the river. I was sure it would be cold. But it's not.

My ghost melts into the water and the world welcomes me home.

How to Feed a Stranger's Donkey

by

KATE NEWMANN

The donkeys had moulty coats
and long eye-lashes and
the softest nose-breath
and warm reaching lips.

You had to keep your palm level,
your fingers glued together. You had to
make your hand a flat platter to hold the apple,
not let it arch up like a frightened animal.

Each year we came to Cruit
– you say *critch*. We became ourselves
all salt-blown and sand-scoury. Sometimes
Cruit was an island, joined with a bridge.

 Sometimes you could walk across the ridged
 sand and then only the rockpool remembered
 what it was to be stranded. We drew
 and coloured in and knew the names:

wild thyme, sea thrift, lady's bedstraw,
bell heather, bird's foot trefoil, scabius
(we thought of scabby), devil's bit,
eyebright, sheep's bit

and one day the donkey bit
Beverly's finger. An accident.
They didn't always look as if they liked you.
But the donkey's monumental teeth,

its vast slobbery gums,
could bite right through the core
and whole body of an apple.
This was an accident.

Beverly's finger turned the colour of harebells
and there was blood. Beverly screamed
like a storm-full of herring gulls and black-backed gulls
and oyster catchers and curlews and terns.

She sat on my mother's knee and keened.
She was given the last – the only –
purple winegum. And I felt a wave, no, a tide,
rise in me. Me – an only child –

without knowing the word for it,
discovered sibling rivalry. I wished
it was my finger that had been bitten
accidentally by the donkey.

The Library Cat

by

SARAH WEBB

Tim did not like the Library Cat and the Library Cat did not like Tim. The first time he tried to pet her, she hissed and raised a paw at him. When Tim told his mum what had happened, she said, 'That grumpy old thing – don't mind her, she doesn't like anyone. She's what they call a feral cat. She lives in the wild. She's not tame like Tiger.'

Tiger was Tim's cat. Tim's dad had moved to Galway just after Christmas and had taken Tiger with him. 'Sometimes mums and dads stop getting on,' his mum had explained. 'It's nothing to do with you, I promise. We both love you very much.' Tim didn't really understand. If that was true, why was his Dad living so far away now?

Tim and his mum were living with his nan now. Even though Tim had begged, Tiger couldn't stay with them because cat hair made his nan come up in hives and sneeze like a demon.

His dad came to visit him once a month but it wasn't the same. Tim missed his old life. He missed the garden with the tyre swing. He missed his bedroom and the star stickers on the ceiling that glowed at night.

But most of all he missed Tiger. It wasn't fair! He had no-one to play hunting with in the garden. No-one to be a zombie when he acted out Minecraft. No-one to tell his secrets to. Tiger was his best friend.

Tim's mum worked in Dalkey Library. She also looked after the Library Cat. Every day she opened the door to the walled garden, filled her bowl with cat food and gave her fresh water to drink. It was called the Maeve Binchy Garden after a famous writer who used to live near by.

'The Library Cat is getting fat,' she told Tim one evening. 'I'll have to stop feeding her so much.'

The next time Tim visited the library he went straight to the glass door and peered out into the walled garden.

'Where are you, Library Cat?' he said.

He waited but she didn't appear. He was just about to turn away when he spotted a flash of orange in the tall spiky grass by the back fence.

It was the Library Cat. And his mum was right about her getting fat: the base of her belly was curved like a moon. Tim sat down beside the glass and watched her. She padded towards him, but this time she didn't raise her paw. She watched him back.

Tim stared into her golden eyes and missed Tiger even more. He felt so sad he had a pain in his stomach. Maybe the Library Cat would let him pet her. He stood up and opened the door but the Library Cat ran away.

Tim stepped into the garden. The roses were out and the air smelt sweet. He walked towards the fence, his feet crunching on the gravel.

'Library Cat,' he called. 'Here, puss, puss, puss.' That's how his mum always called her.

He thought he sounded a bit stupid and he was about to stop and go back inside when he heard a rustling. The Library Cat stuck her head through the grass and stood there, looking at him.

Tim started to walk towards her, slowly. 'Here, puss, puss, puss.' He put his hand in front of him and wiggled his fingers, the way his mum did.

The Library Cat
stayed motionless, her eyes
glued to Tim's face. He got nearer and nearer but the Library
Cat still didn't budge. He was standing just in front of her
now, his fingers reaching out towards her.

She vanished into the grass again and this time he followed her. He took a few steps, grass poking under his grey
school trousers and tickling his ankles. The Library Cat was
just ahead of him. Then she stopped and disappeared into a
hole in the ground. Tim knelt down and peered in. The hole
was lined with dry grass and fur.

Tim could see the Library Cat's face, her golden eyes
shining up at him. He jumped backwards in fright. But she
stayed in her earthy home. She didn't take a swipe at him,
not this time.

Tim sat there, his eyes fixed on the hole. He stayed so still
that he could feel his heartbeat thumping in his ears. And
then he heard something, a soft mewing noise. A little nose

poked
out of the
hole and then another. Two
tiny kittens, no bigger than his hand. One was
almost pure white, with orange and brown markings on her
paws, like she was wearing socks. The other was a tabby cat,
just like the Library Cat.

'Are they your kittens?' Tim asked her. 'Do they have names? How about Socks, because of the socks, and Binchy, after the writer lady?'

The Library Cat tilted her head. He took this as a yes.

He heard his mum calling him from the doorway.

'Better go,' he told the Library Cat. 'I'll be back tomorrow.'

The next day was Saturday. Tim's mum was working, so he asked his nan to take him to the library. While she sat and read the newspaper, Tim went outside to find the Library Cat.

At the entrance to the hole he said, 'Here, puss, puss, puss.'

The Library Cat slid out, followed by the kittens. They blinked in the light and the tiny tabby sneezed.

'Bless you, Binchy,' Tim said, and then laughed at himself. He didn't know if you were supposed to bless a cat.

He took a tiny knitted mouse on a string out of his pocket and placed it on the ground. It was one of Tiger's favourite toys. Then he pulled on the string and the mouse moved forward. Socks ran after it and caught it with her paw.

'Good girl, Socks.'

Tim tugged gently once more and the kitten let the mouse go. She followed the toy along the ground with her eyes and then pounced. Tim pulled it gently out of her paws and placed it in front of Binchy.

'Come on, girl,' he said. 'Your turn.'

But Binchy wasn't interested. She just looked at the mouse and then sneezed again.

Tim left the mouse with Socks and went to fetch their food and water. When he came back, Socks was lying on her back, chewing on the toy's head while the Library Cat watched her. Binchy was curled up on the ground, fast asleep.

Tim put the bowls down beside the Library Cat. She hesitated for a moment before sniffing the food and then starting to eat. It was the first time she'd eaten in front of him. Usually she waited for him to move away before she'd touch her food.

'Tim? Are you out there?' It was his mum.

He stood up and walked through the grass towards her.

'What are you doing?' she asked.

'Looking for grasshoppers.'

His mum looked confused. 'Grasshoppers?'

He nodded. 'We're doing them in school.'

On Monday, Tim found it hard to concentrate in class. He kept worrying about Socks and Binchy. Maybe he'd made a mistake. Perhaps he should have told his mum about them. He hoped they were OK.

After school, his mum said he could walk to the library on his own as it was only down the road. Stepping into the walled garden, he smelt roses again and sniffed in the sweet air. It was a lot better than the classroom stink of egg sandwiches and brown bananas.

'Here, puss, puss, puss,' he said.

This time the Library Cat meowed from the back of the garden. He followed the noise. She was lying in the grass, Socks and Binchy curled up against her tummy, sleeping.

'Hello, girl,' he said. 'I was thinking about you and the kittens all day.'

The Library Cat looked at him and blinked a few times as if she understood what he was saying.

'I have a cat called Tiger but she doesn't live with us any more. Dad moved to Galway and he took her with him.

I miss her a lot. Nothing's the same now. Mum's always so busy with work and Nan just has this stupid concrete yard so I can't play football or anything.'

Tim told the Library Cat more about his dad. He told her about Tiger and the games they used to play together. Then he told her about school and the Cutest Pet competition. He explained how they had to take a picture of their pet and the class got to vote on the cutest animal.

'Sally-Ann Heaney's cat won,' Tim told her. 'Fluffy. And she isn't half as cute as Tiger. Teacher said I could enter Tiger if I wanted, even if she lived in Galway, but I didn't feel like it.'

Tim heard a noise behind him. It was his mum. She was sitting on one of the benches in the garden.

'Who are you talking to?' she asked.

'The Library Cat.'

She smiled. 'I'm sure she's a good listener.'

Tim went to the library every day that week. Every time he called 'Here, puss, puss, puss,' the Library Cat meowed back at him.

He played with Socks and the toy mouse. He tickled Binchy's tummy and rubbed the soft fur on her back and under her chin. He wasn't sure she'd let him at first, but she seemed to like it. And the Library Cat didn't swipe at him once. They were friends now, but she still didn't let him pet her.

The kittens were getting bigger and bigger. They were different – Socks was lively and brave; Binchy was quiet and timid. The Library Cat still kept them hidden from view but Tim wondered if his mum suspected something. She'd started to leave more food out than normal, and he often found her sitting in the garden after his daily chats with the Library Cat.

One Friday three weeks later, Tim visited the walled garden after school as usual. He called, 'Here puss, puss, puss,' but there was no answer. He tried again, but still nothing. He walked through the grass – no Library Cat, no kittens. He crouched down and peered into the hole. Two small golden eyes stared back at him.

'Binchy,' he said softly, not wanting to scare her. 'Come here, girl.'

She crept forward. He put out his hand and she sniffed it. He moved backwards and she followed him out of the hole. She allowed him to pet her, giving a small little purr that made her back tremble.

'Where's your mum?' he said. There was still no sign of the Library Cat or Socks.

Tim wasn't sure what to do. He couldn't leave her, not all alone. Then he heard a voice behind him.

'I think the Library Cat's left her behind, poor wee thing.' It was his mum.

'Will she be OK on her own?' Tim asked.

She sighed. 'I doubt she'd survive very long. She's not a fighter, like her sister.'

'You know about Binchy and Socks?'

His mum smiled. 'Great names. And you've been doing a brilliant job watching out for them. I think the Library Cat may have left her behind on purpose.'

'What do you mean?'

'I think she wants you to take care of Binchy and it might just be possible. I've found a house, and this is the best bit – it has a garden.'

Tim's eyes lit up like fireworks. 'When can we move in?'

'Next weekend. Your dad's coming up from Galway to help. And guess who's coming with him?'

'Tiger?'

'Yes. For good.'

Tim grinned. That was the best news ever. 'I hope she likes Binchy.'

'They'll be great pals. You'll see.'

Tim's mum was right. Tiger was a bit suspicious of Binchy at first, sniffing the kitten and walking around her, but after a few minutes, she seemed to accept that Binchy came with the new house. When she padded out the back door to explore the garden, Binchy followed her. Soon they were like old friends.

A few months later, Tim was sitting in the library doing his homework when his mum leaned over his desk.

'There's someone in the garden to see you,' she said.

He went outside and there she was, her head poking out of the grass. She looked thinner and her paws were muddy, but it was definitely the Library Cat.

'Here, puss, puss, puss,' he said, putting out his hand. She padded towards him and stopped just in front of his fingers.

'Binchy's doing great,' he said. 'And guess what? We had another Cutest Pet competition and Binchy won.'

The Library Cat meowed as if she understood and then she did something she'd never done before: she rubbed up against Tim's legs and let him pet her. Then she ran back through the grass and over the fence. Into the wild.

The World's Greatest Greatest Teen Detective

by **DEREK LANDY**

Detective Inspector Dempsey stood in the middle of Rush Garda Station, drank his coffee and waited to be hit by a sudden bolt of keen insight. This morning, like every other morning, keen insight failed to strike.

Annie walked over, her light footfall disturbing not one sheet of paper on the floor, not one overturned chair or trashed computer screen. She held another cardboard cup of coffee out to Dempsey. He took it, gave her his empty in exchange.

'He's here,' she said.

Annie went to help Ryan document the damage, and Evan Pearse shuffled in. Despite the coffee, Dempsey relaxed at the sight of the boy. Fifteen years old, yet to reach his growth spurt and sporting a delicate array of spots across his chin, Evan surveyed the scene with a lack of interest that bordered on Zen.

'Evan,' Dempsey said warmly, 'good of you to come.'

'Mum made me.' Evan's tone was sullen. He was in one of *those* moods.

'Oh,' said Dempsey.

'I was playing X-Box. I was on a record-breaking kill streak.'

Dempsey checked his watch. 'I didn't think you got up this early.'

'Haven't been to bed yet. Don't want to sleep. When I close my eyes I just see dying enemy soldiers.'

'Right ...'

'I'm doing my best not to blink.'

'Well, we all appreciate you coming out here to help.'

Evan grunted. 'There was a traffic jam.'

'Yeah,' said Dempsey. 'I heard about that. Some idiot who hadn't taxed his van tried to avoid a Garda checkpoint, ended up crashing into someone else. Minor injuries, but nothing too –'

'I passed it. It delayed me.'

'Well, like I said, we appreciate you coming out.'

Evan grunted again, shoved his hands in his pockets.

'Did your mother tell you what happened?' Dempsey asked.

'Only thing she ever tells me is to tidy my room. I need to move out, get my own place.'

Dempsey frowned. 'You're fifteen.'

Evan rolled his eyes. 'Whatever. What happened here?'

'Someone broke in, assaulted Sergeant Boyle. He's in hospital, nasty concussion, but he's not the one I'm worried about. Garda Paul Casey was on duty last night as well. He's missing.'

'This place is trashed. I bet any CCTV footage has been wiped. What were they after?'

'Well, that's just it. We won't know for sure until Boyle gets back, but it doesn't look like anything's been taken.'

'Apart from a guard.'

'You think Casey's been kidnapped?'

'Obvs.'

'Obvs?'

'Obvs. *Obviously.*' Evan sighed. 'God, you try to use language a little more efficiently and you end up having to explain everything to old people.'

'I'm thirty-five.'

'Two guards on duty in a small coastal town,' said Evan. 'Perpetrator, or perpetrators, sneak into the station, render one guard unconscious and snatch the other one. That clear enough for you? They search for something. Maybe they find it, maybe they don't. Whatever. Anything else happening around then?'

Dempsey said, 'Annie, do me a favour?

Find out if anything else happened in town last night. Break-ins, thefts ...'

'Sure,' Annie said, and flashed Evan a smile before she moved off.

Evan blushed madly and turned away, then froze. His head tilted. Dempsey followed him, watched as he lay down to examine the carpet.

'What is it?'

'Sand.'

'Seriously? How did you see that?'

'Just did. My eyes aren't dried out from old age.'

'Again, Evan, I'm thirty-five.'

Evan got to his feet. He looked glum.

'What's wrong?' Dempsey asked.

'We have to go to the beach,' Evan said. 'I hate the beach.'

Rush had Dempsey's favourite beach. Every summer when he was a kid his family would rent a caravan in Hilly Skilly and spend weeks here, swimming in the sea, running in the dunes, eating ice-cream and growing up in an Ireland that seemed a far away place now. Some things had improved. Some hadn't.

'The way of the world,' Dempsey muttered.

'What is?' Evan asked as they walked onto the sand. There were two joggers and three dog-walkers sharing the beach with them. Annie was hanging back with Ryan at the car, talking on the phone.

Dempsey smiled. 'Just talking to myself.'

'I talk to myself sometimes,' Evan said. 'Mostly to tell the voices in my head to shut up.'

'You are a strange and scary boy, Evan.'

'That's what my teachers say. Tell me about Garda Casey.'

Dempsey shrugged. 'I don't really know a whole lot about him. He was born around here, good with the locals. Engaged to a very nice girl from a very nice family. They might have a bit of money. You think that's why he was kidnapped? For a ransom?'

'Doubt it,' said Evan. 'Does he drive a Blue Opel Astra?'

Dempsey stared. 'How did you know?'

'I'm looking at it.'

Dempsey turned. In the distance, across the beach, was a small carpark with a single car.

They started walking towards it. Annie joined them.

'Sir, the only things reported last night were a fight outside a pub on the main street and a disturbance on East Wall Road,' she said. 'An abandoned house was broken into.'

Evan murmured something.

She looked at him, raising her eyebrows. 'Sorry?'

He blushed, and seemed annoyed by it, like his face had let him down.

'Any damage?' he asked.

'Broken windows, kicked-in doors, a few holes bashed into walls,' she said. 'No-one's overly upset about it – it's due to be torn down anyway to make room for a new apartment block.'

Evan murmured something else that the breeze snatched away.

'Sorry, Evan,' said Annie. 'Didn't quite catch that?'

She stepped closer to the boy, and Dempsey could have sworn he saw Evan's knees melt.

Evan tried to repeat what he'd said, but only managed a high-pitched squeak. He cleared his throat.

'I said, did the station have anyone in the cells last night?'

'One of the drunken idiots from the pub,' said Dempsey, reading through his notes. 'Vince O'Laughlin. Local boy. He got in a fight with a Mr Niall Beshoff.'

'Has Vince O'Laughlin been in trouble before?' Evan asked, ignoring Dempsey and focussing his question on Annie.

'He's got a criminal record,' she answered, 'but nothing too bad. His older brother, now, he's a hard case. He's just been put away for fifteen years. Bank robbery.'

'Donal O'Laughlin,' said Evan.

Annie favoured him with another beautiful smile. 'What a memory you've got, Evan. I swear, you are the most *useful* person I have ever met.' Evan looked at his feet and mumbled and Annie went to walk away, but paused. 'And hey, thanks for fixing up the garden yesterday. You did a really amazing job. My boyfriend's useless at that stuff.'

'Yeah,' murmured Evan. 'And he's cheating on you.'

Her smile vanished. 'Why do you say that?'

'I saw him.'

'You *what?*'

Evan glanced at her. 'I didn't want to say anything. Didn't want to upset you. But he shouldn't be cheating on you. That's wrong.'

Her glittering eyes turned hard, and she turned to glare at Garda Ryan. She stalked across the sand towards him.

Dempsey raised an eyebrow.

'Her boyfriend's cheating on her, eh?'

'Probably,' said Evan.

'So you *didn't* see him?'

'Didn't have to. Read his body language. He's hiding something from her, something he feels guilty about. We'll know if I'm right any second now.'

Back at the squad car, Annie fired off a few choice words Dempsey couldn't hear. Ryan looked stunned. They argued. He fell to his knees, his hands clasped in front of him. She ignored his begging and strode away, leaving him to break down, sobbing.

'You were right,' said Dempsey.

'Usually am,' said Evan.

A text message came through on Dempsey's phone. He read it.

'I'm being sent over a list of people who might have wanted to hurt Boyle. It's a short list, apparently.'

'Wasn't about Boyle,' Evan said, resuming the walk towards Paul Casey's car. 'I was wrong. Not a kidnapping. Last night, Garda Casey parked here. He walked the length of the beach with a second person – those are their footprints – approaching the station from the rear and avoiding any CCTV cameras.'

Dempsey peered at the ground. 'How do you know these are their footprints? They could belong to anyone.'

'Tide's done its best to wash them away, so they're not fresh, but they're still visible, which means they're not that old. I'd say they were made about seven hours ago, around the time the station was broken into. But there's only one set of footprints that make the return journey. So where is Garda Casey?'

'I have no idea.'

Evan rolled his eyes again. 'Course not, that's why you called me. You suck as a detective, but at least you're smart enough to call in someone who knows what they're doing.'

Dempsey sighed. 'You have got to work on your charm, Evan.'

'Don't need charm. I got swagger.'

Dempsey suppressed a grin as they reached the car.

'We'll get a guy down here to open her up, but I don't know what –'

Evan picked up a heavy stone and smashed the driver's window.

Dempsey jumped back. *'What are you doing?'*

Evan reached in, pulled the release for the boot. 'Rescuing a cop.'

He led the
way to the back of the
car and they looked in at Paul
Casey, in full uniform, with his hands
tied behind his back and a gag in his mouth.
Casey blinked up at them. Evan pulled the gag away,
then stepped back.

'Someone hit me from behind,' said Casey, licking his dry
lips. 'They stuck me in here.'

Dempsey moved to help him out, but Evan held up a
hand. 'Wait.'

'My legs are numb,' said Casey.

'Tell us where it is.'

'Where what is?'

'The money. The loot. The swag.'

'I ... what? I don't know what you're talking about.'

'I have to confess,' said Dempsey, 'I don't know what you're talking about either.'

'Garda Casey here is a crooked cop,' Evan said.

'How dare you!' Casey cried, trying his best to straighten out indignantly. It was a futile effort. 'I was assaulted last night!'

Evan's posture changed. Dempsey had seen this before. The boy's shoulders squared and his back straightened. Even his voice changed, became clearer, started biting into each word.

'You're getting married soon, aren't you? Marrying a lady who is used to a certain lifestyle. Must be hard to deal with that pressure. I'm no expert on relationships. I'm only fifteen. I'm not as experienced as I'd need to be to correctly estimate how hard it'd be to say no to an opportunity like this, an opportunity that came your way courtesy of your old friend Vince O'Laughlin. You *are* friends, right? You both grew up around here, after all. How long have you two been buddies?'

'I don't know who you're talking about!'

'Vince,' said Evan. 'You know, the guy in the cell. Your best friend.'

Casey looked beyond Evan, to Dempsey. 'Detective Inspector, please help me out of here.'

'Vince O'Laughlin's brother Donal was involved in a daring bank robbery three years ago,' Evan said. 'They escaped with a lot of money. And I mean, a lot. His two accomplices were arrested within a week. Donal managed to stay free a bit longer – long enough to hide the loot. The money was never recovered, and Donal was caught and sent to prison.'

'My spine is crooked,' said Casey. 'If you don't get me out of here now, I think it might stay that way.'

'Maybe Donal let it slip to his brother where he had hidden the cash, or maybe Vince worked it out by himself. Either way, when word came through that the abandoned house on East Wall Road was to be demolished to make way for a new development, Vince didn't have time to waste.'

'I have no idea what any of this is about,' said Casey.

Dempsey frowned. 'The bank money is hidden in that house?'

'Obvs. But Vince didn't know where exactly, so he had to go through the entire place slowly, methodically. That was bound to attract attention, of course, so he needed to do it at night. And he needed an alibi.'

'Why?' Dempsey asked. 'We didn't know the money was hidden there, so we wouldn't have known if he'd found it.'

'Not an alibi for the cops,' Evan said. 'An alibi for his brother. From what I've read, Donal O'Laughlin is not a man you want to steal from, so Vince got himself very publicly arrested.'

Dempsey's eyes narrowed. 'And he needed a guard to help with that.'

'To arrest him,' Evan said, nodding, 'to release him for a few hours in the middle of the night, and then to return him to his cell by morning.'

'No,' said Casey. 'That's not what happened. I was in the station last night and someone hit me.'

'I'm sure Vince *did* hit you,' said Evan. 'Enough to cause a bruise, maybe even a bump. But that was after you'd found the money, wasn't it? Only Sergeant Boyle heard you upon your return, and he came to investigate.'

'And that's when you hit him over the head,' Dempsey finished.

'No,' said Casey. 'No, sir, that's not what happened.'

'You trashed the place, of course,' said Evan, 'to make it look like whoever assaulted the Sergeant was after something else. And right before Vince locked himself back in that cell, you tied that gag around your mouth, had him tie your hands behind your back. Then you came back here and climbed into the boot of your car.'

'I was dragged here,' said Casey. 'I was barely conscious.'

'Then we'll see that footage on the CCTV cameras, will we?'

'I remember hearing waves,' said Casey. 'I think they took me along the beach.'

'There aren't any drag marks in the sand, Garda Casey.'

'The tide washed them away,' Casey said angrily.

'You've got sand residue on your shoes and nowhere else. You weren't dragged. You walked.'

'Sir, please, come on …'

'Where's the money?' Dempsey asked.

'He doesn't know,' said Evan.

Dempsey noticed the look of surprise on Casey's face.

'He thought he knew, but he doesn't. Vince O'Laughlin double-crossed him.'

Casey couldn't help it. 'What are you talking about?'

'He never intended to split the money with you,' Evan said. 'He needed to make a spectacle of himself last night, something that would stick in everyone's heads. He needed people to see him get arrested so that word would get back to his brother. So he pretended to be drunk.'

Casey didn't say anything.

'But you didn't stop to think about who he was pretending to get drunk with, did you? The guy he had that fight with outside the pub?'

Dempsey flicked back through his notes. 'Niall –'

'Beshoff, yes,' said Evan. 'Of Beshoff's Interior Decorators. He drives that nice yellow van. Vince told him where he and Garda Casey were going to stash the money, and Mr Beshoff collected it a few hours later. But then he encountered a Garda checkpoint, panicked, tried to avoid it and crashed – which led to the traffic jam that delayed me getting here.'

Dempsey took out his phone and punched in a number. 'The van from the checkpoint,' he said. 'Beshoff's Decorators. I want it searched.'

He hung up, and looked down at Casey. 'Anything you want to add, Mr Casey, before we find a bag or two of stolen money in that van? Co-operating with the investigation will help you when this comes to trial.'

Casey hesitated. 'It was all Vince's idea.'

Dempsey sighed, and signalled to Annie. She came over and they hauled Casey out of the boot, replaced the rope around his wrists with handcuffs, and Annie took him away. Casey yelped a lot. Annie was in a bad, bad mood.

'Can I go home now?' Evan asked. His shoulders were slumped once more.

'Sure,' said Dempsey. 'Evan, thank you. I wouldn't have been able to do this without you.'

'Obvs.'

Hands back in his pockets, Evan started to shuffle off.

'I heard some folks from Quantico paid you a visit,' Dempsey said.

Evan turned, shrugged like it was no big deal. 'The FBI want me to move to America. Said they'd train me.'

'What'd you tell them?'

'Said I'd put them on the list. Scotland Yard have been trying to get me to go over there for years.'

'Ah, I suppose I knew it was only a matter of time before someone lured you away from us. And there's nothing we could offer you to make you stay?'

'Nope.'

'That's a shame. Still, maybe that's where you belong – solving crimes for the big boys, taking on serial killers and master criminals. There is probably nothing we have that would entice you in the slightest. I mean, it's not like you'd stay in Ireland simply to meet Annie's younger sister.'

Evan froze. 'What?'

'You didn't know she had a younger sister?' Dempsey asked. 'Well, I suppose that doesn't really surprise me. When it comes to Annie, all you notice is *her*. Everything else kind of fades into the background, doesn't it? Her sister is around your age. The spitting image of her, most people say. Though I happen to think Sonia is *prettier* than Annie. And she's a smart one. Not as smart as you, but then –'

'Who is?' Evan said automatically.

'Exactly. But Sonia's quick-witted. You'd have your hands full with her – *if* you were here. But like you said, the FBI and Scotland Yard are knocking down your door, so I reckon I'll just admit defeat. Hey, I'll let you get back to your X-Box, OK? Thanks again, Evan.'

Dempsey started walking back across the beach. He counted to ten, then glanced back. Evan was still standing there, eyes down, a pensive look on his face.

Dempsey grinned. *Got you.*

ABOUT THE AUTHORS

Pat Boran is a poet, fiction writer and broadcaster and the editor/publisher at Dedalus Press. He has published more than a dozen books of poetry and prose, most recently *Waveforms: Bull Island Haiku* (2015). A member of Aosdána, he was born in Portlaoise but has long since lived in Dublin.

Seamus Cashman founded Wolfhound Press and was its publisher until 2001. He edited *Something Beginning with P*, Ireland's best-loved anthology of poetry for children, and is himself a poet. *The Sistine Gaze* (Salmon Poetry 2015) is his fourth poetry book. He is from Cork and lives in north County Dublin.

Eoin Colfer is one of Ireland's best-known writers for children. His Artemis Fowl series is world-famous and is soon to be filmed. His other books include *Benny and Omar* and the historical adventure *Airman*. He has also written *And Another Thing,* a sequel to Douglas Adams's *Hitch-hiker's Guide to the Galaxy*. Eoin is currently Laureate na nÓg. He is very proud of being from Wexford, but he has lived in various places, including Dublin.

John Connolly is best known for his Charlie Parker thrillers for adults. He also writes the Samuel Johnson supernatural novels for younger readers, and is co-author, with Jennifer Ridyard, of the science-fiction series for older teens entitled *The Chronicles of the Invaders*. John is a Dubliner.

Roddy Doyle

is best known for his Booker-prize winning novel *Paddy Clarke Ha Ha Ha* and his Barrytown trilogy for adults (*The Commitments*, *The Snapper* and *The Van*), but he is also a writer for children. His children's titles include *The Giggler Treatment* and *Greyhound of a Girl*. He is a Dubliner.

Marie-Louise Fitzpatrick

is both a picturebook artist and a writer of novels and stories for older children. She has won the Children's Books Ireland (Bisto) Book of the Year on several occasions, most recently for her novel *Hagwitch*. Among her best-loved picturebooks are *You, Me and the Big Blue Sea*, *I am I* and *There*. Marie-Louise grew up in Dublin and now lives in Greystones, County Wicklow.

Mark Granier

published his fourth collection of poetry, *Haunt*, in 2015 with Salmon Poetry. His children's poems have appeared in the O'Brien Press anthology *Something Beginning with P* and Little Island's magazine *Castaway*. Mark is a Dubliner.

Derek Landy

is one of Ireland's most internationally successful writers for young people. He is best known for his hilarious Skulduggery Pleasant series, featuring a skeleton detective. Derek is a Dubliner.

Paula Leyden

won the Éilís Dillon award for her first children's novel *The Butterfly Heart*, which is set in Zambia; its sequel, *The Sleeping Baobab Tree*, won the Children's Books Ireland special judges' award. She lived in Kenya, Zambia and South Africa before moving to Kilkenny.

P. J. Lynch

is widely regarded as Ireland's finest illustrator. He has published more than twenty books over his career, among them the much-loved *The Christmas Miracle of Jonathan Toomey* and *A Christmas Carol*. He has won many awards, including the Mother Goose award and the Kate Greenaway Medal (twice). Originally from Belfast, P.J. now lives in Dublin.

Oisín McCann is an illustrator as well as an author of books for children and teenagers. He has written many novels across several genres and is best known for his thrillers and fantasies. His most recent book is *Rat Runners*. He is a Dubliner, with links also to County Louth, but he now lives in County Meath.

Geraldine Mills is an award-winning writer and poet. She has had four collections of poetry published and three collections of short stories, the most recent being *Hellkite* (Arlen House 2014). Her first children's novel will be out soon from Little Island. She is a native of Galway, where she still lives.

Jane Mitchell

has written several books for children and young people. Her first novel, *When Stars Stop Spinning*, was Bisto Book of the Year, and her more recent *Chalkline* won not only a CBI Merit award but also the Children's Choice award. Jane is a Dubliner.

Kate Newmann

published her first collection of poems, *The Blind Woman in the Blue House*, in 2001. Since then she has published *Belongings* (with Joan Newmann), *I Am a Horse* and *Grim* (Arlen House 2015). She is co-director of Summer Palace Press. She facilitates creative writing with teachers, adults and children. She was born in County Down and her home is in Donegal.

Siobhán Parkinson was Ireland's first Laureate na nÓg. She has written almost thirty books, mostly for children, and has won several CBI awards. Her most recent book is *Alexandra* (Little Island 2014), and she compiled *Magic!*, a collection of new Irish fairy tales (Frances Lincoln 2015). Her novels for older children are published by Hodder. She grew up in Galway and Donegal but is mostly a Dubliner.

Jim Sheridan is Ireland's best-known film director. His films include the multi-Oscar-winning *My Left Foot* and *In America*, the second of which he wrote with his daughters Kirsten and Naomi. Jim lives in Dublin with his wife Fran.

Sarah Webb

worked as a children's bookseller before turning her hand to writing. She has written and compiled over thirty books for both children and adults. Her best-known children's books are the Ask Amy Green novels for young teenagers. She is from south County Dublin, where she still lives, and also has family links to West Cork.

Enda Wyley

is a poet and children's writer as well as a teacher. Her fifth poetry collection, *Borrowed Space, New and Selected Poems*, was published in 2014 by Dedalus Press. Her books for children include *Boo and Bear*, *I Won't Go to China!* and *The Silver Notebook*, all published by The O'Brien Press. Enda is a member of Aosdána. She lives in Dublin.

The Once upon a Place Project

Laureate na nÓg brings great children's literature to children, young people and adults around Ireland and gets them enthusiastic about stories, books and reading. The laureate also works to raise the profile of children's literature, especially Irish children's literature, in Ireland and abroad. Our current Laureate na nÓg is Eoin Colfer, an internationally renowned writer of stories for children and young people.

Eoin's major laureate project, Once upon a Place, has been bringing the magic of stories and storytelling to children all over the island of Ireland – to places where a storyteller might never have visited before, as well as to extraordinary locations like a steam train, a lighthouse, a haunted house, where children can have amazing storytelling experiences.

Eoin is a great believer in the power of place to inspire stories, and this book is the result of his invitation to a bunch of great Irish writers and poets to write stories inspired by places they feel close to – their home towns or places they love to visit on holiday or places that were important to them in childhood. That makes this book a central part of Eoin's Once upon a Place project.

The Laureate na nÓg project is an initiative of the Arts Council with the support of the Department of Children and Youth Affairs, Children's Books Ireland, Poetry Ireland and the Arts Council of Northern Ireland.

PREVIOUS LAUREATE NA NÓG PROJECTS INCLUDE

THE LAUREATE INTERNATIONAL LIBRARY – a collection of books from around the world, some in translation into English and some in their original languages (established by Siobhán Parkinson Laureate na nÓg 2010–12)

PICTIÚR – the largest-ever touring exhibition of contemporary Irish children's book illustration, raising the profile of Irish illustrators on the international stage (curated by Niamh Sharkey Laureate na nÓg 2010–12)

Laureate
na nÓg